K19 SECURITY SOLUTIONS
TEAM ONE

—BOOK ONE—

RAZOR'S EDGE

USA TODAY BESTSELLING AUTHOR

HEATHER SLADE

MORE FROM AUTHOR HEATHER SLADE

BUTLER RANCH
Kade's Worth
Brodie's Promise
Maddox's Truce
Naughton's Secret
Mercer's Vow
Kade's Return
Butler Ranch Christmas

WICKED WINEMAKERS
FIRST LABEL
Brix's Bid
Ridge's Release
Press' Passion
Zin's Sins
Tryst's Temptation

WICKED WINEMAKERS
SECOND LABEL
Beau's Beloved
Coming Soon:
Cru's Crush
Bones' Bliss
Snapper's Seduction
Kick's Kiss

ROARING FORK RANCH
Coming Soon:
Roaring Fork Wrangler
Roaring Fork Roughstock
Roaring Fork Rockstar
Roaring Fork Rooker
Roaring Fork Bridger

THE ROYAL AGENTS
OF MI6
Make Me Shiver
Drive Me Wilder
Feel My Pinch
Chase My Shadow
Find My Angel

K19 SECURITY
SOLUTIONS TEAM ONE
Razor's Edge
Gunner's Redemption
Mistletoe's Magic
Mantis' Desire
Dutch's Salvation

K19 SECURITY
SOLUTIONS TEAM TWO
Striker's Choice
Monk's Fire
Halo's Oath
Tackle's Honor
Onyx's Awakening

K19 SHADOW OPERATIONS
TEAM ONE
Code Name: Ranger
Code Name: Diesel
Code Name: Wasp
Code Name: Cowboy
Code Name: Mayhem

K19 ALLIED INTELLIGENCE
TEAM ONE
Code Name: Ares
Code Name: Cayman
Code Name: Poseidon
Code Name: Zeppelin
Code Name: Magnet

K19 ALLIED INTELLIGENCE
TEAM TWO
Coming Soon:
Code Name: Puck
Code Name: Michelangelo
Code Name: Typhon
Code Name: Hornet
Code Name: Reaper

PROTECTORS
UNDERCOVER
Undercover Agent
Undercover Emissary
Coming Soon:
Undercover Savior
Undercover Infidel
Undercover Assassin

THE INVINCIBLES
TEAM ONE
Decked
Edged
Grinded
Riled
Smoked

THE INVINCIBLES
TEAM TWO
Bucked
Irished
Sainted
Hammered
Ripped

THE UNSTOPPABLES
TEAM ONE
Furied
Merried

COWBOYS OF
CRESTED BUTTE
A Cowboy Falls
A Cowboy's Dance
A Cowboy's Kiss
A Cowboy Stays
A Cowboy Wins

Table of Contents

1

Razor

When my best friend sat me down and told me it was time we both grew up, I thought maybe that oughta be a wake-up call. And then when he took it a step further and said he no longer wanted to be called "Paps," like he had been for almost fifteen years, I decided that, maybe, it was time to check the mirror to see if I was getting as gray as he was.

Gunner "Paps" Godet had been my fellow Marine, sidekick, partner in crime, wingman, and confidant since we'd both arrived at the Marine Corps Recruit Depot in San Diego for boot camp. It had been a fluke that Godet was even there. Given he was an East Coast boy, he should've been sent to Parris Island in South Carolina. But his dad was a USMC O-8, also known as a two-star, who oversaw the base at Camp Pendleton, north of San Diego. That meant Gunner had his pick.

I hadn't cared either way, although everybody I served with later, told me how damned lucky I'd been to end up where I had.

"What the hell are you doin' now?" Gunner asked.

Truth was, I was standing in front of a mirror, giving myself a pep talk. It wasn't being a groomsman in our mutual friend's wedding that worried me, or even that K19 Security Solutions—the company Gunner and I owned with two other partners—was morphing so quickly I hardly recognized it anymore. Instead, it was the woman my friend's fiancée had paired me up with in the wedding party.

Avarie McNamara, who I should've forgotten months ago, wound up center stage in every fantasy I'd had when I needed to take the edge off. It didn't help that the one and only time I'd met her in person, she was wearing the hottest damn bikini I'd ever seen.

She'd let me know, in no uncertain terms, that she was interested that day, but I hadn't been able to take her up on it. I'd been on the clock, filling in as her friend's bodyguard long before she knew she had one.

I'd known a lot about Ava prior to her coming on to me that day, but I hadn't allowed myself to get to know her in the intimate way she was suggesting.

"It's a damn tuxedo," Gunner griped, interrupting my thoughts of the gorgeous woman I was about to see for the first time in over a year. "There's one way to wear it. Nobody gives a shit what you look like, anyway. Let's go."

It wasn't unusual for Gunner to be grouchy. I hadn't really known him to be any other way. But in the last six months, it had gotten a lot worse.

I understood why, though. No one else had been under K19's watch for as long as Lena "Barbie" Hess had been. When she went off her rocker, decided to make a deal with some really bad Russian dudes, and then threatened to kill one of our own, Gunner had been forced to take her down.

I rubbed my chest where it still hurt to think about. It had to be so much worse for him. It wasn't just that Gunner was responsible for Lena's death; I suspected that, at some point, he'd fallen in love with our former commander's daughter. He'd never admit it, though, and I respected that.

"What is with you?" Gunner asked when we got in the car and I rolled my shoulders.

"I don't want to talk about it."

I realized that Gunner might be under the impression I was thinking about Barbie too, considering she had been the mother of the woman getting married today.

"Ava McNamara," I admitted.

"Hot little number. Her twin too. How is she a problem?"

"I can't stop thinking about her."

"That's not like you," Gunner muttered.

"You should've seen the bikini she had on, that day on Fire Island."

I'd spent a total of twenty minutes with her, so for her to be on my mind at all was unusual.

But the fantasies? *Shit.* There were times they seemed so real I could swear I knew exactly how her nipples would harden under my touch, and how her wetness would coat my fingers when I sneaked them in her bikini bottom.

I could even remember how she'd smelled that day. At first it was of sand and sun and margaritas, but the longer we'd talked, the more the sweet scent of her arousal eclipsed everything else. That wasn't something I had to imagine; that was a bona fide memory.

When Gunner pulled into the parking lot of San Ysidro Ranch just outside of Santa Barbara, I saw Penelope, another bridesmaid, walking along the pathway between two cottages.

If Ava was wearing the same dress Penelope was, the fantasies I'd been having would soon get a hell of a lot hotter.

The small amount of pale-green fabric she wore was shorter than most bridesmaids' dresses I'd ever seen, with a halter top that left little to the imagination. Ava and her sister, Aine, were far more endowed than this girl. I couldn't even imagine how good the dress would look on them.

Gunner laughed, checking out Penelope like I had. "You're in for it."

I knew it, but then there was always a chance that reality-Ava wouldn't be half as luscious as I remembered her being.

Plus, I knew her type. She was a spoiled little rich girl, looking for someone to take care of her the way Daddy did. I'd known plenty of girls like her. They didn't think much of me until they found out I was a partner in a successful security and intelligence business.

Then there was the other type. They'd take one look at the body I worked so hard to keep strong and fit, decide I didn't have much of a brain, and treat me like a boy toy. I didn't complain, though. It worked to my advantage when they were looking for someone to rock the shit out of their world but didn't expect me to call the next day.

Maybe that's how it would go with Ava later. Wasn't bridesmaid/groomsman sex a thing? After the wedding, she'd invite me into one of these cottages I guessed went for at least a grand a night, and I'd pound her sweet body out of my system.

"You ready?" asked Gunner.

"No," I grumbled, feeling more like I should take my second cold shower of the morning. Ava McNamara was close—soon she'd be close enough to touch—and I had no control over my body's reaction to knowing that.

If I didn't get myself into her tight little body tonight, I'd be able to pound nails with the raging hard-on I got every time her image crept into my brain.

2

Ava

I looked in the mirror for what felt like the thousandth time and touched up my lipstick, feeling more nervous than the bride appeared.

Quinn and Mercer, the groom, were one of those couples who everyone knew were meant to be. I'd known it from the first time Quinn introduced him to me and the rest of our group of friends.

There was no question, even then, that Mercer loved her. I could see it in the way he touched her and smiled at her. I'd been jealous at the time, particularly since I found out only days before that my ex and first love was getting married.

Dash and I had been broken up for over two years, but at the time, I would've rather been the one announcing I was engaged.

I groaned and rolled my shoulders. I shouldn't be thinking about Dashiell Finnegan today or any other day. Not only had I discovered he was a scumbag criminal, the last time I'd seen him, he threatened to kill me if I told anyone what I discovered about him.

Within a few days of me catching him passing information to someone in exchange for cash, he'd been arrested. I heard someone had called in an anonymous tip. Dash probably thought it was me, but it wasn't. It wasn't long after that I'd been contacted and subsequently questioned as a potential witness. I still didn't know how they'd gotten my name, but they had and, unfortunately, that meant I was going to have to testify if his case went to trial.

It wasn't Dash that was worrying me now, though.

"Are you okay?" my twin, Aine, asked.

"I'm fine."

When Aine cocked her head, I took her arm and pulled her away from the others.

"Do I seem nervous?"

"Probably not to anyone else."

Aine was the only one who knew the size of the crush I had on Tabon Sharp—the man Quinn had paired me with for the wedding.

Describing who he was to anyone outside of our group of friends was way too complicated. When we'd first met him, he'd been introduced as Quinn's boss at the non-profit she'd interned for the previous summer.

Later, we found out that wasn't the case at all. It turned out that, unbeknownst to Quinn, Tabon was her temporary bodyguard and was filling in for Mercer, who had secretly been her "protector" for years.

When Aine first told me all of this, my first reaction had been that it was a joke.

"Sounds like the plot of a romance novel. Although, I have to admit I'm not surprised he wasn't her boss. I thought he seemed too young," I'd said when my twin convinced me she wasn't kidding.

"Here's the other thing," Aine had said. "He and Mercer own a private security firm, called K19 something-or-other, with a couple of other guys. And, get this, I guess no one calls him Tabon; his 'code name' is Razor."

As if the man hadn't been hot enough before. His nickname, or whatever it was, elevated him to rock-star status in my fantasies.

The first time we'd met, my four best friends and I were staying at a waterfront house on Fire Island, and had just come off the beach to get a drink. Quinn recognized him first and went to say hello. When she rejoined us, I made a beeline in the direction of the man who had to have been the hottest-looking guy on the island that weekend.

The board shorts he wore were red, almost the same color as my bikini, and his plain white V-neck shirt looked like it might be a size too small. Through the thin cotton fabric, I could see the hard outline of his rock-solid chest in detail and the tribal tattoo that started on his left pec and continued down his chiseled arm, almost to his elbow.

He'd smirked when my eyes finally met his, and offered to buy me a drink. "I like what I see too," he'd said, looking me up and down like I'd done to him.

When his gaze lingered on my bikini top, I'd felt my nipples harden as my body instinctively leaned into him. When he looked up and smiled, I practically melted into his arms.

His dark-brown eyes, almost black like his spiky hair, danced in amusement and crinkled at the corners when he smiled broadly.

If he'd snapped his fingers that day, I would've done anything he commanded me to. He exuded a deep, underlying power that made a lot more sense when I found out he owned a security company than it did when I'd thought he was the chief operating officer of a Manhattan-based non-profit that worked to preserve historic buildings.

"Stop thinking about him," Aine whispered. "Your cheeks are flushed and, um…you might want to wear these." My twin handed me a set of nipple covers.

"I already am," I whispered back.

"Then double up because they aren't hiding a thing."

Could I help it if Tabon Sharp set every nerve ending in my body on fire? It wasn't just that my nipples hardened whenever I thought about him, the rest of my body responded with equal fervor. If I didn't get my hands on that man tonight, I might combust.

3

Razor

Gunner and I walked up to Cottage Twenty, where the groom told us to meet him.

"Good afternoon, Tabon," said Kade "Doc" Butler, father of the bride and one of the K19 partners.

"Just because Gunner has decided he no longer wants to go by the name we've been calling him for almost fifteen years, doesn't mean I'm ready to do the same."

I actually preferred Razor. Tabon was my dad. My grandfather too. In fact, I was the fifth namesake of the original Tabon Sharp. When I was a kid, my dad referred to me as *Five.*

Razor sounded edgy—even dangerous—and that was the kind of life I led. Before my three partners and I formed K19, I'd been one of the most lethal operatives in the NCS—the CIA's National Clandestine Service. My kill count was almost as high as my captures, not that I was proud of it.

The only thing about it that made me stand up tall was that word on the street was not to fuck with Razor Sharp.

"It's about that time, I guess," said Doc.

I watched as the groom, Mercer, approached his future father-in-law.

"Before you say anything," Doc began. "I chose you. Never forget that. My plan was for you to protect my daughter, not fall in love and marry her, but since you did, I couldn't be more elated. I know you'll make her very happy, and hope she does the same for you."

"Thanks," Mercer said, visibly moved by Doc's words. "I love her so much."

"I know," Doc said before turning and walking out the door.

"My brothers better get here soon," murmured Mercer right before the door opened and two men who looked like clones of him walked in.

"Here they are now. This is Owen. Owen, this is Paps—sorry, Gunner, and Razor. And this is my youngest brother, Hudson."

"You're the reason we couldn't have a bachelor party," I said to Hudson, who had flown in from Europe late last night.

"No, he's the reason." Hudson pointed at Mercer.

I'd been giving Mercer's brother shit about it, but the kid was right. Neither Mercer nor Quinn wanted any kind of bachelor/bachelorette parties.

I pulled the wedding bands that Mercer had given me last night out of my pocket and handed them to Owen, the best man.

"These are your responsibility now," I said. While I was usually the one who tried to lighten the moment with a joke, the fact that Mercer had asked me to keep them until Owen arrived, meant something. I was honored, even though it was a little thing.

"Ready?" Gunner asked Mercer.

"Pretty sure he was born ready," I answered for him.

"I love her so much," Mercer said again.

I put my hand on his shoulder. "Hey, buddy, time to come out of the prenuptial trance. You're actually gonna have to say something other than that soon."

Gunner made sure everyone exited the cottage in the right order. I didn't really understand all this wedding shit, but evidently, other than the best man, the bride determined the order of the groomsmen. Didn't seem like a big deal to me until she'd called me aside a couple of days ago.

"I've put you with Ava," she'd whispered. "You know, in the wedding."

"Uh…okay," I'd answered.

"Aine is my maid of honor, so I wanted Ava to be next to her, since they're twins."

I'd nodded even though I didn't really understand what she'd meant. I'd been to weddings, but never realized the order people walked in was planned.

"Does that mean I get to dance with her?"

She'd laughed like she thought I was kidding, but I hadn't been. She had no idea how much I lusted after Avarie McNamara.

4

Ava

Aine was fussing with Quinn's veil while one of the other bridesmaids was handling the sapphire blue earrings Quinn's father had given to her last night.

"These are both old and blue," Quinn said he'd told her. "They belonged to his grandmother. Her name was Analise, which is my middle name," she added with tears in her eyes.

The five of us—Aine, Tara, Penelope, Quinn, and me—had been best friends, calling ourselves the "tribe of five," since we met at boarding school when we were seven years old.

None of us came from ideal families, but Quinn had always had it harder than the rest of us. Until recently, her father hadn't been a part of her life. In fact, she didn't even know him.

Quinn's mother hadn't really been a part of her life either, although more than her dad had been. She'd recently passed away under circumstances Quinn wasn't able to talk about.

"Who chose these dresses?" I asked, trying to position the second set of nipple covers.

Aine motioned at Tara, who looked fabulous in the sage-green halter dress that was cut in such a way that only a backless, strapless, stick-on bra could be worn with. As well-endowed as Aine and I were, we might as well have gone without.

"You're the maid of honor, shouldn't you have had a say?"

Aine ignored me like she usually did when I was spouting off about something we couldn't change.

"Do you see where Mom and Dad are sitting?" I asked when we were outside, waiting for the processional to begin.

"Dad is in the second row from the back, with Kelly, and Mom is…um…oh, Lord…in the second row from the front."

I didn't want to ask what our mom was wearing; whatever it was would be outlandish.

"She's got the spaceship hat plastered to the side of her head."

I gasped. "The bright-purple one?"

Aine shook her head. "This one is pink."

Both my sister and I had inherited our bigger-than-average bosoms from our mother, and while neither of us tried to hide them, we certainly didn't flaunt them the way the woman did who insisted we call her Peggy instead of Mom.

What had Quinn been thinking when she invited our parents? And why couldn't they have simply sent a gift like Tara's and Pen's parents had, instead of both showing up with their spouses?

Peggy, no doubt, would have too much to drink at the reception and suggest she and our dad bury the hatchet and have a dance, to which our father would adamantly refuse while his third—or was this his fourth—wife crossed her arms and pouted.

"Again, you're the maid of honor. You couldn't have talked Quinn out of inviting them?"

Tara glared at me. "Shush."

Once she turned around, I stuck my tongue out. If I was going to be scolded like a child, I might as well act like one.

"Can you see Tabon?" I whispered, trying to be quieter.

"Yes," answered Aine.

"And?"

"And what?"

"How does he look?"

"Like the other five men wearing tuxedos. Actually, that isn't true. Mercer looks the best. Tabon might be the runner-up."

When the music began, my eyes met Quinn's. She looked absolutely gorgeous. Only the death grip she had on her father's arm gave away her nervousness. I smiled, turned back around, and took a deep breath. If I looked at Tabon, would he be looking at me? God, this was ridiculous. He probably didn't even remember meeting me.

I stepped forward after Penelope and Tara started their walks down the aisle, and couldn't help myself; I had to look.

He was looking right at me, wasn't he? Or was he looking behind me? He smiled then and winked, his eyes not wavering as I followed my two friends.

He looked good. He'd shaved the dark stubble I remembered, making his jawline look even more powerful, but his eyes hadn't changed—they still danced when he smiled.

When Aine took her place next to me, all eyes turned to where Quinn stood with her father. Those who were seated stood when the music began.

The sunlight hit my friend's simple lace gown, making it glow. I peeked around Aine, wanting to see the look on Mercer's face. As I'd expected, he was mesmerized.

When they reached the front, Kade moved Quinn's veil from her face, leaned forward, and kissed her cheek.

The minister asked everyone to be seated and began the ceremony. It wasn't long like some I'd attended in New York, where it felt more like mass for five hundred than a wedding. Instead, this was a simple, sweet profession of love, consecrated by God, and witnessed by people who cared deeply about the couple.

I almost cried, which wouldn't have been at all like me. My sister was the weeper and was making good use of the handkerchief she'd remembered to hold around the stems of the flowers she carried.

The minister pronounced them husband and wife, the two kissed, and then began the recessional.

Soon, within seconds really, I would step forward and take Tabon's arm as he escorted me to where the bride and groom now stood.

My eyes met his, and he smiled, holding his arm out for me. "Avarie," he whispered when I took it. How did he know my full name? "You look beautiful," he added.

He felt good at my side. Strong, confident, almost commanding. There wasn't an ounce of self-doubt in this man whose arm held mine.

I remembered Quinn saying that Mercer made her feel cared for and safe. It wasn't long after she'd met him, and she'd sounded so certain. I understood what Quinn had meant now. Just having Tabon by my side made me feel, if not cared for, definitely safe.

5

Razor

It wasn't that I wanted to get away from Avarie—she was delightful—but all eyes were on us, or it felt that way. Soon, the photographer would take pictures, and when he did, there would be hard evidence of how much I wanted the "hot little number," as Gunner had called the woman in the barely-there sea-foam-green dress.

We'd separated after walking back down the aisle to stand beside Mercer and Quinn: guys to the groom's right and girls to the bride's left. Maybe I should've said something more to her, but there'd be plenty of time to talk later, and if I'd stopped long enough to look into her baby-blue eyes, I would've taken her behind the tall hedges that separated one part of the garden from the other and kissed the shit out of her.

Instead, I took my place next to the best man and willed myself to think about anything other than how Ava had felt with her arm in mine.

"How ya holdin' up, Casanova?" asked Gunner when he approached after escorting the final bridesmaid down the aisle.

"I don't know…she seems kind of…" I said when we were far enough away that no one else could hear me.

"What?"

"Young."

Gunner laughed. "For you?"

It wasn't just that she was young. There was a certain doe-eyed innocence about her that belied the party-girl act she'd displayed that day on Fire Island. The good-girl vibe she gave off today was opposite of how I remembered her.

"I don't do good girls."

"Is there some requirement that we *do* the bridesmaids, because I'll tell you what, I'd *do* Penelope in a hot minute."

"What are you, fifteen?"

Gunner smirked. "If I were, I sure as hell wouldn't be complaining about the age difference."

I looked over at the group of bridesmaids. Even though Ava and Aine were twins, there was something different about them that I couldn't define. They both possessed mouth-watering curves, but only Ava's called out to me and made me take notice. Only Ava made me want to pull the pins holding up her sandy blonde hair and let it cascade over her tanned shoulders, only to gather it in my hand and grip it tightly as I took her sweet body from behind.

"We're here another few days," said Gunner. "Ask her out."

"*Out?* For what? A date?"

I didn't do dates. I didn't take pretty girls out for dinner, or for walks on the beach, or kiss them politely at their front door. I offered them a night of off-the-charts, hotter-than-hell sex, and expected them to be long gone by sunrise.

"Hey, boys," said Doc, approaching us with his wife, Merrigan, former MI6, and now managing partner of K19. Merrigan, code name Fatale, had been one of the deadliest assassins in the UK's Secret Intelligence Service, but now, seven months pregnant, she seemed perfectly happy managing the day-to-day operations of their business.

"Nice wedding, Doc," I said. "Quinn is absolutely stunning."

My teammate, and one of my closest friends, beamed. "She is, isn't she?"

I wondered if Doc regretted not being a part of his daughter's life for the last fifteen years. The reason for his absence had been to keep her safe, but there had to be a part of him that wished he'd had the opportunity to get to know her as she was growing up.

Merrigan touched Doc's arm. "The meeting," she murmured.

"Right. I hate to bring up business on a day like today, but I got an urgent call from Striker."

"About?" asked Gunner.

"Asset protection."

Griffin Ellis, code name Striker, was K19's primary contact at the CIA, and was responsible for the majority of work that came into our firm.

"I thought we were closed for business for the next six months," Gunner grumbled.

"We are," said Doc. "Except the asset is practically family. It's one of the bridesmaids."

"Which one?" I asked.

"It might be one of the twins," said Merrigan.

"What are we protecting her from?" Gunner asked.

"I don't know the answer to either question yet," said Doc. "We'll find out when we meet with him later this afternoon."

Gunner and I exchanged a look. The four partners of K19 had decided not to accept any new assignments for at least six months, and even then, we'd agreed to evaluate whether we wanted to extend our moratorium on new business.

If we accepted, I would be the only one of the four available to take it on.

Given Merrigan was pregnant, Doc was out. Mercer had just gotten married, and he and Quinn were leaving on their honeymoon in the morning. As it stood, they had no firm itinerary, nor did they have a planned date when they'd return.

That left two of us, and Gunner was the least ready to take on another job involving asset protection. He may never be ready to do that type of work again. Which meant I would be it. What if the twin who needed protection was Ava-of-the-hot-red-bikini? How in the hell would that work?

"Say no," said Gunner when Doc and Merrigan walked away.

"Is that really an option?"

"Of course it is. Tell Doc you have a conflict of interest."

I scrunched my eyes. "What if it's the other twin?"

"And what if it's not? Listen to me, tell him you want in her panties too bad to be able to protect her. You don't think Striker has active agents he could assign to this, or even other contractors?"

"There must be a reason he came to us."

"I'm tellin' you, say no."

I got where Gunner was coming from, but the minute Fatale said it was one of the twins, I knew that if it was Ava and she was in some kind of danger, I would never forgive myself if I didn't protect her.

Conflict of interest? Hell, yeah, but my conscience would overrule any logic my brain threw at me. Or maybe it was my heart that would do the overruling.

6

Ava

"Damn, they're hot," said Penelope, walking up to Aine and me.

"Right?" said my sister, looking at Gunner and Tabon like they were pieces of wedding cake.

"You had a thing for Razor, didn't you, Ava?" asked Pen.

I shrugged. A thing? I had a twenty-minute conversation with him; he bought me a drink, and then I spent the last year fantasizing about him. Yeah, that would constitute a thing.

"I've got my eye on the other one, anyway."

"He seems grouchy, Pen," said Aine. "But then you usually go for that type."

"Yep, the broodier, the better, I always say."

I rolled my eyes. Aine was right. Penelope was her own worst enemy when it came to her taste in men. Every one she'd dated, as far back as I could remember, was an asshole in my opinion. Once Penelope set her sights on someone, though, she could be relentless.

"Mercer's brothers are pretty hot," I said, wishing I could convince Pen to go for one of them instead.

"Too boring."

"Mercer isn't boring," said Aine.

"Okay, well, that doesn't mean they aren't. Plus they're both too young."

That was the other thing about Penelope. Unless they out-aged her by at least ten years, they were "too young."

"What are you talking about?" asked Tara, coming back from the ladies' room.

"Ranking the groomsmen on a hotness scale," I told her. "I say Tabon is a habanero; Pen says Gunner's a serrano, and both of Mercer's brothers are sweet bell peppers."

"I totally disagree," said Tara. "Hudson is a Carolina Reaper."

"Ew," groaned Pen. "You always go for those baby-faced little boys."

Tara rolled her eyes. "He's older than we are."

"But a hella lot less mature."

"You're the one ranking their Scoville scale while you stare at them like they're filets."

"Gunner is a porterhouse, not a filet."

I laughed. "And Tabon is a bone-in rib eye."

"We should stop staring at them," said my twin.

"Why? It doesn't look like they're bothered by it."

"They're ready for us," said Tara, pointing at the photographer who was motioning us over.

I tried to walk past Tabon without looking at him, but just like before, I had no willpower where the man was concerned. Maybe this time, he wouldn't catch me ogling him.

7

Razor

I winked at Ava when I caught her looking at me, and immediately regretted doing so. If what Doc had said was true and the K19 team would soon be responsible for her protection, I had to keep our relationship strictly professional.

When she smiled, I shook my head and turned away. Yeah, maybe I'd just hurt her feelings, but it would be far worse if she got it in her head that anything could happen between us.

"Time to pair up," said the photographer a few minutes later. "Bride, groom, best man, maid of honor, and so on."

I inwardly groaned. Why the hell had Quinn matched me up with Ava? This shit would go on all damn day. First, photos, then I'd probably have to sit with her during dinner, and then, I'd absolutely have to dance with her. Would it be terrible if Gunner and I switched? Yeah, probably.

When she came and stood next to me and the side of her boob grazed my arm, I almost jumped out of my tux. As though it had a mind of its own, my tricep moved back and forth, sending zingers straight to my groin.

"Be careful, or I'll have a wardrobe malfunction."

"Wouldn't bother me a bit." Jesus, what was wrong with me? Wasn't my brain communicating with my mouth?

"You might not mind, but Quinn definitely will."

I reluctantly shifted so no part of my body touched the sexy parts of hers. "Sorry," I murmured, moving even farther away.

"No, I'm the one who's sorry," she said, her eyes hooded.

She crossed her arms. Didn't she realize what that did to her boobs? If there was going to be a wardrobe malfunction, that was the surest way to make it happen.

I looked down at her from the corner of my eye and, sure enough, I could almost see her nipples. Wait. Maybe I could see them. But what did she have stuck to them? Were those Band-Aids?

"What are you looking at?" Ava hissed, lowering her arms.

"Is everything okay? You know, here?" I asked, motioning to my own chest.

"What? *Oh my God,* are you serious right now?" she whispered.

"I thought I saw bandages…"

Ava turned the other way, so her back was to me, but I could still see the flush of embarrassment creep up her neck.

"They aren't bandages," she seethed.

I leaned forward. "What are they?"

She turned around and huffed, covering her cleavage with her bouquet of flowers. "None of your business, and stop looking at me."

I grinned, wishing I could. Indignant Ava was damn cute.

When the photographer was finished, I thought about apologizing to her, but she and the rest of the bridesmaids had mysteriously disappeared.

"I'm tellin' you," said Gunner. "You gotta say no."

I felt the same pang I had earlier, hating the idea of anyone other than me protecting Ava, unless it was a woman. Now, *there* was an idea. Maybe we could bring Alegria in. She was one of K19's pilots, but she had asset protection experience. I'd make the suggestion when we met with Striker later.

"Wanna switch?" Gunner asked when we approached the head table.

"What do you mean?"

"You're seated between the twins, and I'm between the other two. We could switch, and then you won't embarrass yourself, looking like you want Ava for lunch instead of whatever crappy wedding food they serve."

"You don't think Quinn would mind?"

"Hell, no. Look at her. You think she has anything on her mind besides making babies with Eighty-eight?"

"You talk too much. Have you always been this way? *Jesus,* just shut up."

Gunner walked away, laughing, and I watched as he switched the place cards. Something in my gut told me this was going to come back to bite me in the ass.

Penelope leaned over and motioned for me to get closer. "You're a dick," she whispered.

"Not the first time somebody's called me that."

"Her ex used to pull shit like this, and even he wouldn't have humiliated her at a wedding."

"Humiliated her? What the—"

"You know what? Just shut up."

I didn't bother looking in Tara's direction to see if she was judging me equally harshly. Fortunately, Gunner was keeping her busy, talking about God knew what. I was grateful, though, especially knowing how much my friend detested small talk.

From where I sat, I couldn't see Ava, but what the hell was the big deal? Did it really matter where any-one was seated?

Shortly after we'd finished eating, the bride and groom made the rounds of tables, thanking their guests, and I stood to go talk to Ava.

I sat back down when I saw her engaged in conver-sation with both of Mercer's brothers. She was talking in an animated way and smiling.

"I thought you were switching with me, not Hudson," I said when Tara and Penelope left the table.

"Changed my mind. I wanted a better vantage point. Plus, I'm thinkin' of havin' a little party of my own with those two."

"Who two?"

"The bridesmaids."

It was hard to know whether Gunner was serious or not. If he was, I hoped the women were smart enough to shut him down.

"She didn't look happy about you switching seats. I think you hurt her feelings," said Gunner.

"Me? You're the one who moved the place cards."

"Yeah, but you wanted me to."

Had I? *Shit,* even I wasn't sure.

"Want another drink?" I asked. I sure as hell needed one, and I wasn't interested in another person telling me I'd hurt Ava's *feelings*, particularly my own best friend.

"I'm good," Gunner answered.

"Looks like you're stuck with me," Penelope said a little while later when we watched Mercer's youngest brother escort Ava to the dance floor, while his older brother danced with her twin.

"Should I cut in?" I asked.

Penelope laughed. "Tara already dislikes you. Ava's pissed, which means Aine is too. I'm the only one of the tribe—other than Quinn—who's still speaking to you. I wouldn't advise alienating me too."

"Tara dislikes me?"

"That was all you got out of what I said? How about, 'how can I make it up to Ava?'"

"Let's dance." I grasped her hand so we could join the rest of the wedding party.

Dancing was something I knew how to do. Foxtrot, waltz, two-stepping, line-dancing, even tango—it didn't matter what type of music played, I could dance to it.

I held Penelope in my arms, all the while trying my hardest not to watch Mercer's little brother put the moves on Ava.

They looked comfortable—smiling, chatting, and dammit if that didn't make me miserable.

"I heard that," said Penelope.

"What?"

"You just growled."

I laughed out loud. "Did I, really?"

She nodded. "A girl knows when you aren't paying the slightest bit of attention to her. She also knows when you are, even if you're dancing with someone else."

"Sorry." I focused my attention on the woman in my arms instead of the woman who wasn't, at least until I saw Ava and Hudson leave the dance floor. His arm was around her waist as he led her into the gardens.

8

Ava

I was the last to arrive at the table, other than Quinn and Mercer, thankfully, but was confused about where I was supposed to sit. The only empty seat, other than the bride's and groom's, was between Mercer's two brothers. When I'd checked the table earlier, Tabon's place card was next to mine. Instead, he was sitting on the opposite side, between Penelope and Tara. Evidently, he'd switched his seat.

I plastered a smile on my face, struck up a conversation with Mercer's two bell-pepper brothers, and tried to forget Tabon Sharp existed.

After twenty minutes of painfully awkward small talk, I decided they weren't even in the pepper family; they were more like cauliflower or broccoli, both of which I detested equally.

I peeked over my shoulder and saw Tabon's gaze follow us as Hudson led me away.

"It's really beautiful here," I heard Mercer's brother say.

"It is. Did you know this is where Laurence Olivier and Vivien Leigh were married?"

"Who?"

"You know, Laurence…never mind." There was no sense in repeating the names; it was obvious Hudson had no idea who I was talking about.

"You sail, right?" he asked, walking up the steps to a gazebo with a view of the Pacific Ocean.

I nodded. "Raced an F3 when I was in college."

"Cool."

"And you?"

"Yeah. Raced all my life."

Good Lord, this was painful. Mercer's brothers were sweet, but neither were engaging conversationalists. I turned to suggest we go back to the reception, when he pounced.

Before I realized what was happening, he had his arm around my waist, holding me far too tightly, and his tongue was fighting its way into my mouth.

"Hudson, *no.*" I put my hands on his chest and pushed as hard as I could, but he was rock solid.

"You heard the lady say no, *asshole.*"

"Hey, Raze, no harm," Hudson said, backing away from me with his hands in the air.

I watched as Tabon got in Hudson's face.

"I'm not going to spoil your brother's day with this, but if I find out you've ever disrespected a woman—any woman—again, you'll deal with the full force of K19."

Disrespected. That word resonated. Hudson had forced himself on me, but Tabon had disrespected me too when he switched his seat. I walked down the steps, murmuring my thanks, but not at all interested in either of the apologies they were trying to offer.

"Hey, Mom…I mean…Peggy," I said, joining my mother and sister. "Where's Paul?"

"He went to get me another drink."

Great, just what my mother didn't need. It was only one in the afternoon, and she already seemed drunk.

"Quinn and Mercer should be cutting the cake soon," I said, not that I expected it to make any difference. Once my mother had one drink, she wouldn't stop until she passed out. It was a train wreck Aine and I had witnessed too often when we were growing up.

"Aine mentioned you were thinking of staying in California a few more days."

"We are."

"Oh," my mother said, looking at my twin, "I thought it was just Ava."

"Both of us were talking about it," Aine told her.

My mother's eyes scrunched. "I'd planned to invite you to join Paul and me at the shore."

"I never said it was just Ava. I always intended to stay too."

"I must've misunderstood." She looked miffed, but I didn't care. Neither Aine nor I spent much time with her, not since we were little girls. If we'd ever been important to her, she would have dealt with her alcoholism.

9

Razor

"What's happenin'?" asked Gunner, handing me a beer.

"Eighty-eight's little brother had his hands all over Ava, so I set him straight."

"What did Ava say when you interrupted her romantic tryst?"

"The first thing she said was no, and that wasn't to me; it was to that little shit, Hudson. She didn't say anything at all to me, because, evidently, we aren't speaking."

"I was thinking about heading home tomorrow, but maybe I'll stick around for a few days. This will be entertaining."

"Please go home," I muttered, walking away.

The woman I saw Ava and her sister talking to reminded me of that character, the one that was half human, half octopus, in the mermaid cartoon movie my nieces liked so much. The only difference was, the character looked like she weighed three hundred pounds, and this woman couldn't tip the scales at much more than one hundred, and half her weight had to come from her boobs.

Her hair, which stood up on end like mine did, was pure white. Her eyes were coated with bright blue and purple eye shadow; she wore flaming-red lipstick, and the dress she was wearing looked to be at least a size too small.

I might've laughed, until I saw the mortified look on Ava's face when I approached. Instead, I took an entirely different tack.

"Who is this beautiful woman?" I asked, taking a seat next to Ava.

"This is my mother, Peggy," she answered. "Mom, this is Tabon."

"Most people call me Razor," I said, smiling at Ava. "I like it when she calls me Tabon, though."

The woman held her hand out to me, palm down, as though she expected me to kiss the powdery-white back of it. Instead, I shook it and put my arm across the back of Ava's chair.

From the corner of my eye, someone else caught my attention. I looked over at a man and woman who had turned around and were walking the opposite way. There was something about the man that raised my hackles.

I glanced over at Gunner, who appeared as affected as I was.

In our line of work, trusting our instincts was everything. When my radar reacted that strongly, it wasn't something I could ignore.

"That was my dad," Ava said, noticing where I was looking. "And his latest wife."

My mind raced with the intel K19 had on Ava and her twin sister. Surname: McNamara. Father's name: Conor. Recently married for the fourth time to Kelly. Maiden name: Fitz-something. Conor was in the import-export business, worth a cool hundred-mil at least. The new wife was barely out of high school.

Ava's mother had also remarried, to Paul Whitely. Fitting name, given the pallor of her skin.

Nothing had ever turned up on either of the parents, certainly not at the level of my reaction.

"Tabon? Is everything okay?" Ava asked.

"Yeah, yeah. Everything's fine. Just thought I saw a ghost for a minute."

"You look like it."

I leaned over and kissed her cheek. "Be right back."

Gunner and I both walked toward the man and woman.

"Did you get a good look at that guy?" I asked.

"Nah, I was hoping you did."

"Just caught the back of him, but damn, I got icicles."

"Me too. I'll circle around and check him out."

"He's Ava's father, Conor McNamara."

"The hell he is," I heard Gunner say as he walked away.

While my teammate went to give the man another look, I went in search of Doc, whom I found seated with Merrigan.

"There he is," she said, when I leaned in to kiss her on the cheek. "Kade tells me you've been romancing one of the bridesmaids."

"You know not to believe everything you hear, Fatale."

I'd meant it as a joke, but I saw her eyes flicker for just a moment. Evidently, something in my words struck a nerve. It wasn't the use of her code name; everyone referred to her as Fatale on a regular basis.

Within a couple of seconds, though, she was back to her radiant self. Doc ran his hand lovingly over his wife's protruding stomach.

"Got a minute?" I asked right about the same time Gunner joined us.

"Tell you what, boys, I need to find the loo, so I'll leave you to chat." Merrigan kissed Doc's cheek. "You can fill me in later," she said as she walked away.

Gunner and I told Doc about our reaction to seeing the twins' father. While I couldn't place him, and neither could Gunner, we both knew there was something sinister about the man.

"He almost reminds me of somebody, but I can't figure out who," said Gunner.

I felt the same way, but I was certain I'd never seen him before.

One thing everyone knew about me was that I never, ever forgot a face. If I'd seen someone even for a split second and they'd been identified, I could pull that memory up twenty years later, and be able to report who the person was, where I'd initially seen them, and give a brief but concise background report. It was my superpower.

Gunner nudged me. "Better get back to your girlfriend."

"Ava? I don't know where she is," I said, distracted by the man seated at a table across the lawn.

Gunner motioned with his head. "She's where you left her. Maybe you should rethink your career as a spy, dude."

10

Ava

I'd been watching Tabon long before his eyes found mine.

He, Gunner, and Quinn's dad had been talking about my father, and I wanted to know why, particularly when I saw the looks on their faces.

"Had you and Dad ever met Quinn's parents?" I asked my mother.

"When would we have?"

"I don't know, maybe when they first brought her to school."

"Good Lord, Ava, that was years ago. I have no idea."

"Think, Mom. Do you remember anything about when Quinn arrived?"

"I don't. Why do you ask?"

"I thought maybe Daddy knew Quinn's father."

"I don't think so. Not that he ever told me anything."

I recognized my mother's tone. What she really meant was that my father never told her about all the other women he slept with while they were still married.

"Oh, look, Razor is coming back. That is one fine-looking man, Ava." My mother fanned her face.

"Can I talk to you for a minute?" he asked, rejoining us at the table.

My mother nudged my shoulder. "Go with him," she whispered.

I stood and stalked away, hoping Tabon would get the hint that I wasn't interested in talking to him.

"Hold up," I heard him say but I kept walking.

There were several things that had bothered me so far today, not just that I sensed he and his friends were talking about my dad.

Sure, I had a crazy, mad crush on him, but when he'd switched his seat at the head table, he'd hurt my feelings. Why did he want to talk to me now?

Plus, as my mother said, Aine and I were planning to spend more time in California, particularly since Quinn and Mercer were planning to live here.

If I became his wedding hookup, wouldn't it be horribly awkward running into each other when he was with his friend and I was with mine?

I had to admit I'd come on pretty strong the day I talked to him at the bar on Fire Island. I'd all but offered myself to him. At the time, my bravado had been fueled by a combination of alcohol and a broken heart. I wasn't sure I actually would've delivered if he'd taken me up on it. That wasn't the kind of girl I was. In fact, I hadn't had sex with anyone before or after Dash.

"Avarie, stop."

I did. I don't know why. There was just something about his voice. I didn't move until he was by my side.

"Come with me," he said, pulling me through an archway in the hedge that led to another grassy area. I gasped when he spun me into him and captured my body against him with his arm around my waist.

"I have wanted to do this for so long." His lips descended on mine, and his tongue pushed its way between them. He cupped my cheek with one hand while he dug his fingers into my waist with the other.

Unlike Mercer's brother, I welcomed Tabon's kiss. I wrapped my arms around his neck and kissed him back.

11

Razor

Kissing Ava was everything I'd dreamed it would be. Our tongues tangled together as she rubbed her body against mine.

The noise, the other guests, even the voices in my head melted away until all that remained was the soft, sweet woman in my arms. I dropped my hand from her waist to her ass and kissed my way down her neck, over her collarbone, to the place where the halter top of her dress barely covered her breasts. Soon, I hoped I'd feast on their bareness, but for now, I needed her mouth again.

Ava's hands were in my hair, pulling until my scalp tingled. She whimpered when I ran my tongue back up her neck, scattering kisses along the way. My lips met hers again, and I nipped the bottom one when she didn't open to me fast enough.

"Do you have any idea how much I've thought about you this last year, wishing I could get my hands on you? Wishing I knew how it felt to kiss you?"

Ava's lips were swollen, and her cheeks had turned the prettiest shade of pink where my whiskers had rubbed against them. Her eyes were downcast, and I didn't like it one bit.

"Look at me," I demanded. "Have you thought about me, Ava?"

She took a deep breath and bit her lip. "Tabon, you can't just *do* this."

"I can't ask if you've thought about me?"

"No, I mean…just because Quinn 'put us together,' doesn't mean I'm your date. You can't just kiss me, or drag me away from the wedding, or…*kiss* me." Ava looked behind her, making sure no one was paying attention to her raised voice. Her eyes bored into mine, and I met her gaze, waiting for her to say more.

"I'm the one that can't do this," she finally said.

"Can't do what?"

"I can't have sex with you, Razor, and just walk away tomorrow. I'm not a hookup kind of girl—"

"You know you're feeling the same thing I am."

"No," she said, pushing away from me. "I'm sorry if I misled you or gave you the impression that I was yours for the taking. I'm not. I had too much to drink that day, and…other things were on my mind. If you want to know the truth, I barely remember meeting you—"

I grasped her nape, so tempted to cover her mouth again with mine, force her lips apart with the tip of my tongue. Instead, I pulled back and looked into her eyes.

"I'm sorry if I embarrassed you earlier when I switched our seats. I thought…hell, I don't know what I was thinking."

"I spent four years with a man who humiliated me every chance he got, and I vowed I would never allow anyone to do that to me again."

"I won't. I promise."

"Don't make promises you can't keep, Razor," she said as she walked away.

The thing I hated most, of everything she'd said, was that she'd called me Razor. No one called me Tabon, and that was my choice. But when she did, it felt right. Why did I love the way it sounded on her lips?

"Gentlemen," said Doc, approaching Gunner and me later when the wedding reception was winding down. "Come with me."

We followed him and Merrigan to the cottage they'd booked at the resort, and saw Striker standing right outside.

"I'm sorry about the timing, but this couldn't wait."

Once inside and seated, Striker laid it out for us.

"Ava McNamara is a witness in the upcoming trial of her former boyfriend."

My head spun. I'd *known* it was Ava who would be needing our protection. "What did he do?" I asked.

"A whole slew of crimes, but we've got him for insider trading, money laundering, and investment fraud."

"Wait a minute. All of this is under FBI jurisdiction," Gunner said. "Why is the agency involved?"

"There are a couple of reasons. First, we believe someone from the FBI is in on it. Second, we have evidence that the scope of the organization he works for is far-reaching."

"Meaning what, exactly?" I asked.

"Internationally."

"Are we protecting the asset from the boyfriend, or from someone else?" asked Gunner.

"Someone else."

I stood and ran my hand through my hair. "Who?"

"We can't say yet."

"You can't say, or you don't know?" Doc stood like I had. "That's what I was afraid of," he said when Striker didn't answer.

"Why do you need Ava's testimony?"

"She witnessed an exchange. We also believe she unknowingly has a connection to the organization."

"If you want us to take this on," Doc snarled, "you need to tell us everything you know, and everything you don't. I'm not sending one of our guys in on this unless we're fully briefed."

Merrigan stood and put her hand on Doc's arm. "May I?" she asked Striker, who nodded.

"MI6 has been on this longer than the agency has," she began. "CRM Allied, an Irish export company with very hard-to-trace ties to Azerbaijan, has been on our radar for the last five years, but we haven't been able to find enough to go after them. Dashiell Finnegan, with whom Ava McNamara had a relationship, was recruited by someone close to her. However, it was probably the worst decision CRM made."

"We believe Finnegan knows enough to bring the entire organization down," added Striker.

"Where is he now?" I asked.

"In custody, but under protection."

"Who else knows about Ava's involvement?"

"The man we believe controls CRM," answered Striker.

"For fuck's sake." I was getting sick of him dragging this out.

"Ava McNamara's father," said Striker, who shrugged when Merrigan scowled at him.

"Jesus," I muttered. "And you're saying he knows she's a witness?"

Striker nodded. "There is little doubt that Finnegan made him aware of Ava's involvement."

I looked at Merrigan. "How long have you known this?"

"Wait a minute—" said Doc, but for the second time, Merrigan rested her hand on his arm.

"I didn't. The McNamara family was never on our radar. Or, how should I put this? MI6's investigation was of someone whom, now, I'd say is operating under a fake identity."

"Who have you been investigating?"

"Makar Petrov."

I sat back down and rested my head in my hands. Petrov, a black market arms dealer, had disappeared over twenty years ago, rumored to have been killed and dumped in the Caspian Sea; his body was never found.

There was no intelligence naming his killer, but when I'd heard the story, I figured it had to be CIA. The man was as evil as they came, and had been responsible for selling weapons to countless rogue factions from several different nations who all had one thing in common—they hated the United States with every breath they took.

"What about the other twin?" Gunner asked. "What does she know?"

"It was suggested to Ava that she not divulge what she knew to anyone, particularly her sister. Given it would put Aine in danger, she agreed."

"And the mother?"

"From what we can tell, she has no idea that she married a Russian mobster twenty-two years ago. Petrov, if it is in fact him, obviously underwent a great deal of plastic surgery. We also believe he killed the real Conor McNamara and took on his identity."

"What evidence do you have?" I asked.

"Only that McNamara was listed on a flight manifest, traveling one way from Dublin to New York City, within a few months after Petrov was reported dead.

Prior to marrying the twins' mother, McNamara had no family who might've reported him missing."

"I meant that McNamara is really Petrov."

"We don't, but we hope to very soon."

"How?"

Striker held up a bag containing a toothbrush. "DNA."

"How'd you get that?"

"Housekeeping."

I shook my head. "Do you already have Petrov's?"

"MI6 does," answered Merrigan.

I turned back to Striker. "What's the plan? Why'd you come to us?"

"It's a close-cover assignment," he answered.

"Got anybody in mind?"

"You know I do, Razor."

"Why me?"

"Because we believe Ava McNamara would be open to a…relationship with you."

"No, I won't allow it," said Doc. "It isn't how our team operates."

Striker raised an eyebrow. "I didn't realize you alone called the shots," he said, looking first at Doc and then at me. "Razor?"

"I'm in," I answered, refusing to look at anyone seated at the table before I stalked out.

"You sure about this?" Gunner asked, following me outside.

"Yeah. I'm sure."

"It means lying to her."

I knew that. There was no way Ava would go along with witness protection unless she knew the full story, which at this point, I couldn't tell her. Until we could prove her father wasn't who he said he was, and could bring him down, Ava would have to be kept in the dark.

"No," said Doc, joining us outside. "As I told Striker, I won't allow it."

"And as Striker said, it isn't your decision, Doc."

"You're telling me that your intention is to seduce my daughter's best friend and pretend to be involved with her for God knows how long?"

"Who says I'd be pretending?" I walked away. I knew Doc wanted to follow me. I also knew Gunner wouldn't let him.

"It was a beautiful wedding," I overheard Ava say to Quinn.

"You keep Razor on his toes," Quinn winked when her eyes met mine. "Seriously, though, I think the two of you are well suited."

I walked up behind Ava. "Got a minute?" I whispered.

"No." She walked away but I followed. "What do you want?" she asked when I caught up and rested my hand on her shoulder. "I thought I made myself clear earlier."

"I have an offer to make you."

When Ava rolled her eyes and folded her arms, I did my best to keep my eyes level with hers and not look at the way her dress barely covered her breasts.

"Just listen. This doesn't have anything to do with me. I heard you and your sister were planning on spending a few more days in California."

She nodded. "Pen and Tara are thinking about it too."

"I'd like to offer you a place to stay."

Ava laughed. "With you?"

"No, not exactly."

"Explain yourself, then."

I smiled. Damn, I liked this woman. "I have a place a couple of hours up the coast, in Cambria. It's near where Doc's family lives."

Ava rolled her eyes.

"Wait. Hear me out. It's a duplex. Each side sleeps six, although two of you would have to share a bedroom since there are only three."

"Where would you be?"

"On the other side."

"Why?"

"Why what?"

"Why are you doing this?"

I stepped forward, close enough to tuck an errant strand of hair behind her ear. "Because I want to get to know you better, Ava."

"So there are strings."

"Absolutely not."

She shook her head. "Not interested."

I cupped her face with my palm. "Please."

"Don't do this to me," she said, shaking her head again.

I leaned forward and kissed her forehead. "Please," I repeated.

Her eyes were closed and she leaned into me. She could say she wasn't interested, but her body told a different story.

"I need to talk to the girls."

"Where are they?"

"The cottage."

"I'll walk you there." I took her hand in mine and Ava stopped walking.

"Tabon?"

"Yes, Ava?"

"Is this just a game to you?"

I put my arm around her shoulders and pulled her closer.

"No, it isn't. I can't forget you, Ava, and believe me, I've tried."

"What if I don't feel the same way about you?"

"My heart will be broken, but I'll live. And in the meantime, I'll get to spend some time getting to know the most beautiful woman I've ever laid eyes on."

She huffed. "For now, I'll consider your offer and talk it over with my sister and our friends. But don't push it, Tabon."

I kissed her hand. "I'll be waiting to hear from you. I'm in Cottage Fourteen."

"How'd it go?" Gunner asked when I walked into the bar.

"Fine, I think."

"She's staying at the duplex?"

"She's talking it over with Aine and the other two, but I have a feeling they'll agree to it."

"Shit," groaned Gunner.

"What?"

"You, sleeping next door to four hotter-than-shit young women. You'll have them all to yourself while I go and see my parents."

"I'm only interested in one of them."

"You're only *pretending* to be interested in one of them."

Gunner had it wrong, but if I admitted exactly how interested I really was in Ava, I knew my friend would go straight to Doc, and maybe even Striker, and tell them that I'd already crossed the line and wasn't fit for this assignment.

"I gotta get back to the cottage. She's going to call me there."

"Roger that," said Gunner, raising his glass of beer. "Wait," he said when I turned to leave.

"Yeah?"

"Be careful, Raze."

12

Penelope and Tara were sitting on the floor of the cottage's main room, talking to Aine when I walked in.

"Holy shit," exclaimed Pen. "What is going on with you and Tabon?"

I brought my fingertips to my lips, remembering the way he'd kissed me earlier. "I'm not sure."

"Where is he?"

"Waiting to hear from me."

"About what?"

I looked at my sister. "You know how we've been talking about spending another week or two here?"

"We are too," said Pen.

"He's offered us a place to stay."

"Us or you?" asked Tara.

"Us. He has a duplex in a place called Cambria."

"That's where Quinn was for a while," said Aine. "She said it's really beautiful."

"Anyway, he said we could stay in one side of it."

"Where will he be?" asked Pen.

"The other side."

"Oh. That's disappointing. He didn't invite you to stay with him?"

"I think it's what he wanted, but I would've said no."

"Why?" asked Tara.

"How embarrassing would it be if he kicked me out the first night, after he was done with me."

"What…are…you…talking…about?" asked Pen, needlessly enunciating every word.

"There is no question that Razor is a player."

"That may be true," murmured Aine, whose eyes met mine. "But Tabon isn't."

"Before I call him, I want to go say goodbye to Mom and Dad," I said to Aine.

"Where are they?" she asked.

"I have no idea. I'll call Dad. You call Mom, I mean, Peggy."

Aine rolled her eyes. "I always get stuck with Peggy."

"Dad is heading to the bar," I said after I disconnected the call.

"Mom is *in* the bar."

"Oh, no," we said at the same time, hurrying in that direction and hoping to waylay our father before both of our parents caused a scene.

Aine pointed. "There he is."

"Thank God," I muttered.

"Hey, Daddy," said Aine, catching up with him first.

"There's my beautiful girl. I was wondering if I was going to get to spend some time with you today." He turned to me. "And you too, Ava, what a treat!"

"Where's Kelly?" Aine asked.

"Napping," answered our father, rolling his eyes. "Too much sun or something. I was on my way inside to get a gin and tonic."

"It's such a beautiful afternoon; let's sit outside," I suggested.

"If there's an outdoor bar, that'll work," he responded.

"I haven't seen one, but I'll go get us all something to drink and bring it out."

"Perfect." My father pulled out his wallet.

"I got it, Daddy." I turned to go inside and instead walked straight into a wall of hard-as-rock muscle.

"Whoa, where are you hurrying off to?" Tabon asked, putting a hand on each of my arms.

"Um…to get some drinks for…um…our dad." I motioned with my head to where he sat with my sister.

"I'm guessing you already know your mother is inside."

"Yes," I mumbled.

"I'll walk you in."

"I can handle it."

"I'll help. By the way, what did you decide?"

"We're in," I said, waving at my mother and Paul before going up to the bar.

Tabon leaned forward. "I'm so glad," he murmured. "I have another suggestion."

"Here we go."

He laughed. "How about if I take the drinks out to your father and sister while you spend a couple of minutes with your mom. That way she won't wonder why you ran off so fast."

"She's probably too drunk to notice."

"You may be right, but if you do as I suggest, you'll be more apt to avoid a possible confrontation."

"Thank you."

He kept his hand on the small of my back as we waited for the bartender to make our drinks.

"Are you sure you can take all three?" I asked, since he'd ordered one too.

"Not a problem, sweetheart."

"I won't be far behind. If she thinks I'm with you, she won't want to keep me."

Tabon brushed my forehead with his lips. "You *are* with me."

13

Razor

I had no trouble juggling the two gin and tonics since Aine had ordered a glass of wine. I slipped my sunglasses on, picked up the drinks, and followed Ava over to where her mother sat.

"Hey, Mom. I came to say goodbye."

"Mom?"

"Sorry. I mean, Peggy. Tabon and I are leaving."

"I'll be outside, sweetheart. I'll see you in a minute." I motioned with my head in that direction.

My suggestion that I take the drinks out to her sister and father wasn't exactly selfless. It would give me an opportunity to talk with the man who'd set alarms ringing throughout the K19 team and could very well be Makar Petrov.

"Hello, Aine," I said, approaching them. I handed her the glass of wine, and then turned to her father. "Hello, sir. You must be Mr. McNamara. Tabon Sharp, I was one of the groomsmen, and I believe this is yours."

The man stood and I handed him the drink.

"Where is Ava?"

"Dad, I have to be honest with you. We didn't want you to go inside because Mom is in there," said Aine.

"I see," he said, brushing his finger over his upper and lower lip and studying me.

"She shouldn't be long."

McNamara nodded; his eyes hadn't left my face.

"Who are you again?" he asked.

"Dad, he's one of the groomsmen. He and Mercer—"

"Go way back. We served in the Marines together."

"Hey, Daddy," said Ava, joining us. "I see you've met Tabon."

"How drunk is your mother?"

Ava sighed. "Very."

"I'm not surprised."

I downed the rest of my drink, that was, by request, all tonic and no gin.

"It was nice meeting you, sir," I said. "Sorry to run, but I'll be leaving in about a half hour and still need to pack."

My eyes met Ava's, and she nodded, checking the time on her phone.

"When do you have to leave for the airport, Daddy?"

"I need to be going as well." He kissed each of his daughters and then turned to me.

"Did you say your name was Tabon?" he asked, offering his hand to shake.

"That's right."

"Interesting name."

"It's a family thing."

McNamara nodded and then turned back to the daughters. "Let me know when you plan to be in the city. We'll have dinner."

"Interesting man," I commented once I was certain their father was far enough away not to hear me.

"Our dad has always been…intense," said Ava.

"He works a lot," added Aine. "But you probably know that, don't you?"

I shook my head. "No."

I looked at Ava, who had an odd look on her face.

"Everything okay?" I asked.

She nodded. "Are we following you, or are you planning to give me the address?"

There was a weird tone to her voice, almost as if she was annoyed with me.

"Why don't you ride with me, and Gunner can take Aine and the other two girls?"

"No. That won't be necessary. We have our own car."

Her voice remained clipped, which puzzled me.

"Yes, I know. And I don't. I rode here with Gunner. If I ride with you and the rest ride with him, you won't get lost."

"I don't think so," she said, folding her arms *again*.

I wished she would hurry up and change out of the damn dress that sent my blood rushing to my groin.

"I'll go with you and Razor," offered Aine. "Pen and Tara can ride with Gunner."

Ava nodded, but she sure didn't look happy about it.

"Fill us in on meeting the twins' father," said Doc when he and Merrigan joined Gunner and me in our cottage.

"Every nerve ending tells me that man is dangerous. He definitely suspects that I'm not on the up-and-up, maybe just with his daughter, but he watched me closely."

"We'll know soon enough if he's Petrov, but whether he is or not, he's the head of CRM Allied, and that is whom we're officially investigating. It's CRM that

Ava will indirectly testify against at Finnegan's trial. In the meantime, I can guarantee the agency is making a deal with him to take down the company he works for," said Merrigan.

"What's the status of the daughter?" asked Doc.

"Ava, her sister, and their two friends will be staying in the duplex in Cambria."

"For how long?"

"As long as necessary."

"And if she insists on leaving?"

"I'll handle it, Doc. You do your part of the job, and I'll do mine."

I was getting damn sick of Doc treating me like an employee rather than an equal partner. Sure, he'd always assumed the role of leader, but we'd managed without him when he disappeared for two years.

"Penelope and Tara are riding with you. I'll ride with Ava and Aine," I said to Gunner, who rubbed his hands together.

"Behave," said Doc.

Once this assignment ended, I planned to have a sit down with him, Merrigan, Gunner, and Mercer, and set Doc straight about how decisions were going to be made in the future.

"We gotta go," I said to Gunner, rolling my eyes when my teammate rubbed his hands together a second time.

"You need to settle down, my friend. You're gonna scare all of 'em off." Not that I would actually think that was a bad idea. It might even be considered public service if I warned them about Gunner.

I walked to the girls' cottage while Gunner drove the car closer. I would've preferred having Ava all to myself, but at least she'd agreed to let me ride with her after Aine offered to join us.

"Hey," she said, opening the door when I knocked.

"Ready?"

"Yeah," she answered, "although there's been a slight change of plans."

I felt a pang in my chest. "What?"

"Aine has decided to go with Pen and Tara too. I guess Gunner offered to take them wine tasting on the way to Cambria."

"Would you like to join them?"

"Would you?"

I stepped forward and bent down to look in Ava's eyes. "I asked what you'd like to do."

"Honestly, I'd rather not, which is why my sister said she'd ride with them."

"Are you hungry?" I asked once we were on the road.

"I guess. Although I don't have much of an appetite."

She was back to not looking at me and keeping her arms crossed in front of her.

"Mind if we stop?"

"Do I have a choice?"

And…the brat was back. What the hell had happened after I'd talked to her father that pissed her off?

"I guess you don't," I teased.

"Then, why ask?"

"How old are you?"

"Why do you want to know? To humiliate me? You know exactly how old I am. You probably know my bra size and when I had my last menstrual cycle."

"Nah, but I do know when you lost your virginity." I'd meant it as a joke, but the look on her face indicated she didn't take it that way.

"That subject is off-limits for you. Understand?"

"I was kidding."

"How old are you, Razor?"

"Don't call me that."

"Don't call you an old man?"

Who was crossing the line now? Although she did have a point. I was lusting after a nubile young woman ten years younger than me.

"Don't call me Razor. I haven't told you how old I am."

"Why not? Everyone calls you that."

"Because I want you to call me Tabon."

I pulled off the road when I saw the sign for a brewery that was one of my favorite places to eat.

"Maybe I should call you Mr. Sharp. Or, how about sir? Is that what you're into?"

"That's enough," I muttered before getting out to open the passenger door for her.

"Sorry, sir." She looked down, but with a smirk I wanted to kiss off her face.

"Knock it off."

"Oh, wait. Maybe you want me to call you 'master' instead."

"You aren't funny," I said, feeling heat rise in my cheeks.

"Wait a minute. Is that really what you're into?"

I was tempted to spin her around, press her up against the car, and let her know exactly what I was into. If she didn't shut up, that's precisely what I'd do.

"Don't play with sharp objects, little girl. You're likely to get cut."

"You remind me of my father sometimes."

Those words hurt far worse than if she'd slapped my face. Instead of reacting, which was what she was after, I pretended to ignore her.

I held the door open, and she shimmied her tight little ass inside the brewery. While what she'd suggested wasn't at all what I was into, her bringing up sex of any kind left a definite impression on my cock.

She'd appeared surprised that her comment about her father didn't get the response she'd been going for. Sure, it reminded me that I'd kill the bastard if he laid a hand on either of his daughters, but if she was suggesting we were similar in age, that hadn't bothered me.

Age didn't make a damn bit of difference to me. Older, younger, didn't matter. If two people were attracted to each other, wanted each other, that was all that was important. And right now, I wanted her about a thousand times more than the ice-cold beer I was about to order.

I handed the menu to Ava. "What do you like?"

"I'll have the Mirror Pond Pale Ale, please," she said to the bartender when he approached.

"Can I see some ID?"

When she pulled it out of her purse and handed it to him, the bartender gave me a once-over.

"What the fuck?" I said under my breath. Did I really look that much older than her? "Tell me what you're thinking," I said, noticing the smug look on her face.

She motioned toward the man pouring our glasses of beer. "Clearly, he thinks you're too old for me."

"Do you think I'm too old for you?"

Her cheeks flushed.

"You'd be right," I said when she didn't respond.

We were near the end of the bar, so it was easy for me to twist her around so her back was to the wall in the hallway. I held her face with one hand and circled her waist with my other arm. My lips crashed down on hers. Ava whimpered and ground her pelvis against my cock. I already thought I might lose it, and then she made it so much worse.

"Tabon," she breathed. I could feel her nipples harden against my chest and her pulse speed up.

All I could think about was getting Avarie out of her clothes and under me. My blood throbbed through my veins at the thought of being inside her, her warmth wrapped around me. But we were in a bar at least two hours away from where we were headed. I groaned and took a step back from her.

"Was that just to teach me a lesson?" she asked with hooded eyes.

"What do you think, Ava? Do you think I'm playing games with you?"

"No," she murmured.

"That's right. I sure as hell am not." I took her hand and led her back to the bar. "Sure you're not hungry?" I asked, pushing the food menu toward her.

"Not really," she answered.

"Eat anyway."

When the bartender came back, Ava ordered a pretzel, two prime rib sliders, and a side of loaded tater tots.

I ordered fish tacos.

"I thought you weren't hungry," I said when the man walked away.

"Changed my mind. I do that a lot."

"Yeah, what else have you changed your mind about?"

Ava leaned forward so her mouth was next to my ear. "I no longer think you're too old for me."

"What do you think now?"

She took a long drink of her beer and then plopped it on the bar. "I think you're hotter than shit, Tabon."

"This is your *duplex*?" she asked when I pulled through the gate after it opened.

I had to admit the place was beautiful, and not necessarily what one might expect from the word she emphasized. A lush Japanese garden surrounded the two connected structures, with koi ponds outside each of their decks. The exterior of the house was dark wood with a clay roof.

"This is *yours*?"

"Don't sound surprised."

"It's just so…big."

I wiggled my eyebrows.

"The *house* is big. I mean, it's nothing at all the way I pictured it. Is this where Quinn stayed when she was here?"

"No, that was a rental. I hadn't bought this place yet. And full disclosure, Gunner owns half of it."

Ava's cheeks turned pink. "The half we're staying in?" she gasped. "Will he be here too?"

I laughed. "He isn't supposed to be. His plan was to head back east to see his folks, who live on Chesapeake Bay. Although, after spending a few hours with three beautiful women, he may change his mind."

Ava's eyes opened wide.

"I'm kidding. He won't change his mind, and even if he does, K19 has another house not far from here where he can sleep."

"Why can't he stay in your side of the house?"

Because I'm hoping I can convince you to stay with me. No, I couldn't tell her that.

"Tabon…"

"What?"

"I can guess what you're thinking."

I moved forward and cupped her face with my palm. I didn't remember ever touching a woman in the same way before, but everything felt different with her.

"I'm not going to lie to you, Ava. I want you in my bed more than I've wanted anything in my life. That doesn't mean I'm going to pressure you, or do anything to make you uncomfortable. Do you understand?"

She nodded. "Should we go inside?"

I led her in the front door of Gunner's side of the house, although no one would be able to tell he spent any time there. Both sides had been professionally decorated, and when we bought the property, we'd negotiated to purchase it furnished.

It wasn't ever intended to be a place either of us lived full-time. We'd decided to invest in Cambria, given the property values had recently taken a dive because of the severe drought, which led to an equally severe water rationing. However, as with everything else, it wouldn't be long before the drought ended, and we would be able to turn a profit when we decided to sell.

"It's very *nice*," she said.

"I was just thinking how neither side looks lived in by two single guys. The place came this way."

She walked over to the windows that looked out at the Pacific Ocean. It was an amazing view, but nothing like the one from my house on the Oregon Coast.

Maybe I'd tell her about it and see if she'd like to go there with me sometime. I inwardly groaned, not accustomed to the thoughts that kept popping into my head. What was it about this woman?

"I'll take your bag upstairs, and you can choose your room."

"Okay," she said, hesitantly moving from the window as though I was taking her away from it.

"We don't have to do it this minute."

"It's just that it's so…beautiful. And so different from the Atlantic Ocean."

"Yeah? I haven't spent much time on the East Coast."

"I mean, they're both oceans, but the Pacific has a different vibe."

"That's a good way of putting it."

Ava's cheeks turned pink. "I really do have an extensive vocabulary, and I did graduate from college, although that isn't evidenced by my current conversational skills."

I studied her. "Do I make you nervous?"

Ava shrugged, but then looked into my eyes. "You do."

"Tell you what. I'll take your bag and leave it at the top of the stairs, and you can choose your room whenever you're ready. And then I'll head next door to give you some privacy."

"Oh. You're leaving?"

"I don't have to. Although I should've thought to stop at the market in town. We don't have a lot in the way of provisions."

"I wouldn't mind going with you."

"That would be great. We can pick up whatever you think your sister and friends would like too."

Ava smiled, and I about melted. I moved my hand from her face and rested it on her shoulder, unable to stop touching her. The lure of her lips pulled me in, and I covered her mouth with mine.

When her tongue darted against mine, I groaned and she whimpered. I lifted her legs until they went around my waist, and held her ass with my two hands. I kept my lips on hers, caressing her tongue with mine.

I wasn't thinking about protecting Ava now. She wasn't an asset; she was a woman I wanted.

Thankfully she'd changed out of the dress that had almost driven me mad, but her short-shorts and t-shirt weren't a whole lot better. I could feel the warmth of her arousal as her body pressed against mine, making me increasingly harder.

I turned my head, attacking her mouth from a different angle as she held on tightly. Did that mean she didn't want to let go of me any more than I did her?

I pulled back and looked into her eyes. Her pupils were dilated, her breathing was labored, and her face, neck, and chest were flushed. If this were any other woman, I wouldn't hesitate or ask; I'd take her right where we stood. But this was Ava.

"Talk to me, baby. Tell me what you're feeling."

"You can *feel* what I'm feeling, Tabon."

"Likewise, but we need to talk about this. You just told me I make you nervous."

Ava fidgeted enough that I released her legs. She slid down my body, and I immediately missed her warmth.

"You also make me want you, Tabon."

"Tell me how, Avarie. What do you want from me?"

She tried to hide her face, but I wouldn't let her.

"I need to hear the words, baby."

"I could feel you pulsing against me."

I stroked her cheek with my finger.

"I want that, Tabon. Except I want you pulsing inside me."

I groaned and grabbed her ass with both hands, pulling her body close enough to grind against mine. I was about to pick her up and carry her next door when I saw the lights of Gunner's SUV pulling through the gate.

"We have company," I said, resting my forehead against hers.

"I don't suppose we can sneak next door."

"We could, but we'd have to make it really quick."

She smiled. "We shouldn't."

"You're right. However, I need to do something about this." I pointed to the straining zipper of my jeans.

Ava covered her mouth and laughed. "I'm sorry. Although not as evident, I'm having a similar problem."

I brushed her lips with mine one more time.

"I'm going to carry your bag upstairs, but keep them talking a few minutes before they come up, okay?"

"Uh, okay." She giggled and her cheeks turned that shade of pink I was growing to love.

14

Ava

I watched Tabon's gorgeous ass as he took my bag upstairs. Part of me wanted to tell him to take it next door instead.

"Hello," Gunner called out, opening the front door and sticking his head in.

"Are you waiting for me to invite you into your own house?" I laughed.

"Hope we weren't interrupting anything," he said, coming inside with Aine, Pen, and Tara following behind him.

"You were."

"Oh, damn," said Pen, sounding a little tipsy from wine tasting. "Maybe we should leave."

"They can leave," said Gunner. "There's a whole other side to this place; they can have all the privacy they want." He turned around and winked at Pen. "And so can we."

I wondered if the two were playing or if they were really interested in each other.

"Where's Raze?" Gunner asked.

"Right here, playing bellman," Tabon answered.

"I'm sorry, I could've—"

"Ava, do you really think I would've let you carry your own bag upstairs?"

"Thank you."

"However, I'm off the clock now. Gunner, your shift has started. I'll take my stuff next door, and then Ava and I were going to run to the market."

"We can do that," offered Pen. "As long as Ava drives."

"That's a good idea," said Gunner. "We should talk about—"

Tabon shook his head. Whatever Gunner was about to say, was something he didn't want to say in front of me. I folded my arms and glared at the two men. "Talk about what? My father?"

Tabon looked like he was ready to hurl, and Gunner rubbed the back of his neck with his hand.

"No. Of course not. Um, you'll need these." He handed me the key fob for the rental car.

"Let's get out of here," I muttered to my sister, but not before Tabon could grab my hand.

He pulled me close to him. "Hurry back," he whispered.

"What's wrong?" Aine asked when we walked outside.

"He's lying."

"What about?"

"Dad."

"How do you know he's lying?"

"It's a thing he does. I can't really explain it, but it's the set of his mouth. I wouldn't have thought anything of it, but then I remembered he'd done the same thing when I met him last summer on Fire Island."

"You thought he was lying about something then?"

"He was lying. He was pretending to be Quinn's boss, when really, he was her bodyguard."

Aine shrugged with a skeptical look on her face. "I hope you're wrong," she murmured. "For your sake."

I was just about to start the engine when I saw *Razor* jogging over to the car.

"Miss me already?"

"You know it, baby." He winked.

"What's the real story, Razor?"

"I…uh…remembered I needed to pick something up."

"There isn't enough room for all of us to go," said Tara. "I'll stay here."

"So will I," said Pen.

"There isn't any reason for me to go either," added Aine.

"I guess they figured we want to be alone," he said with a smirk.

"I thought you wanted to talk to Gunner."

"No big deal. We can chat when I get back." He got in the car. "Everything okay?"

"Yep," I answered, not looking at him.

"What just happened?"

"Nothing. Let's just go to the store. I'm tired, and I'd like to get to bed."

"I'm all for that."

"*Alone,* Razor."

He was as quiet as I was on the way to the market. I grabbed a cart when we walked in.

"You can go get whatever it was you needed to pick up," I said, hurrying away from him. I saw him shake his head, but instead of walking away, he followed.

"I'm serious. I don't need help grocery shopping."

"That's clear. I'll tag along anyway."

His voice was as clipped as mine. If he didn't like my attitude, he should refrain from lying to me.

"I thought Gunner was leaving," I said when we stood in the checkout line.

"He is. Although, I'm sure, given the circumstances, he'll stay the night at my place."

I shrugged and took out my wallet when the cashier gave me the total. Razor covered my hand with his.

"I've got this," he said, putting a debit card in the keypad.

"That isn't necessary. I can pay for my own food."

"Yes, I'm aware. However, you're my guest and I insist."

When we returned to the house, Razor suggested I go in ahead of him, and offered to bring the bags in on his own. I almost told him I could help, but changed my mind. I was still pissed about him lying to me, and if that was the game he wanted to play, he'd be doing it solo.

I didn't see anyone downstairs when I went in, so I climbed the staircase.

"That was quick," Pen said when I walked into the first room off the hallway and found her sitting on the bed.

"It's late. Everyone is tired."

"Mm-hmm."

"Where's my stuff?"

"Aine moved it into the room she's in. We figured you wouldn't be staying here anyway."

"You were wrong."

15

Razor

"We got news," said Gunner when I walked into the kitchen and found him sitting at the counter. "It's a match. McNamara and Petrov are one and the same."

"That was fast. You're certain?"

"Lab at Fort Roberts processed it immediately, and since they already had the info from MI6, it wasn't long before they determined it was exact."

I opened a beer, thinking through what Gunner had just told me. Ava's father, who she was obviously closer to than her mother, wasn't at all who he'd pretended to be for the last twenty-plus years. The only thing Conor McNamara had in common with Makar Petrov was neither of them had been able to operate on the right side of the law.

I'd been in this line of work too long to think that someone like Petrov was above keeping his daughter from testifying if, by doing so, in conjunction with Finnegan's turning state's evidence, she could bring down his organization.

Was he arrogant enough to believe no one would find out his true identity? The possibility had to, at the very minimum, be lurking in the back of his mind.

This confirmation meant protecting Ava had escalated to a different level. Not only was I hiding her from someone wanting to stop her from testifying, I would now have to prevent her own father from finding her.

"Are you sure you don't want to step aside and let someone else take over this assignment?"

"Leave it alone, Gunner."

"What about having Alegria take over? You have feelings for the asset. There's no bigger mistake to be made."

"I changed my mind. I'm not walking away from this."

"Roger that," he muttered.

"I swear to God, Gunner, if you go to Doc about this…" I shook my head. "Just mind your own goddamn business. You hear me?"

"I will be talking to Doc about this assignment, Raze, but not in the way you think. The first thing I'm going to tell him is that I'm your number two. Second, you and I will craft a plan *together,* and take it to him and Striker."

Hard as it was for me to consider admitting it out loud, I appreciated Gunner's plan of attack. He was right, I had feelings for the asset, and no one knew better than Gunner how horribly wrong that could go.

"Let's talk tomorrow when we've both gotten some rest. I'll head out to Harmony now," he said.

"You can stay here."

"Not a good idea if you look at the big picture."

Our eyes met.

"You're gonna have to get closer to her, and do it quickly, Raze."

"Fuck," I muttered, knowing he was right. Not just about getting closer to her. He was right about me crossing a line I never should. "Who's in town?"

"We've got a wide selection. We already know Alegria is here. She can be our number three. Monk is here too, and Striker hasn't left yet."

I nodded. "We'll brief Al tomorrow and get her engaged."

Gunner waved behind him as he walked out the front door.

I shut the lights off and slowly made my way up the stairs. I doubted I'd get much sleep tonight; there were too many things I needed to think over.

Gunner's words left me with a bad feeling in the pit of my stomach. If I stayed on her detail, I was going to have to get closer to Ava, and do it fast—which meant this thing between us couldn't happen naturally.

I'd have to lie to her. Our relationship would be based on deception, and that meant it could never be real. Knowing I had to accept that fact, made me feel a profound sense of regret.

"Alegria is in," Gunner told me when he called the next morning. "Any sign of life next door?"

Considering the sun had just come up, I doubted I'd hear anything out of Ava and crew until much later.

"Negative."

"Good. Alegria will head in your direction. When she arrives, you can leave for Harmony."

I knew having her on Ava's detail was a good solution, but the feeling of dread I got from her taking over while I went to Harmony, even just for a meeting, made me sick to my stomach.

If I'd ever wondered how Mercer felt before Quinn knew the true nature of how he'd come into her life, now I could empathize. Mercer had lied to Quinn over and over again. That it was for her protection hadn't mattered. He'd still lied. For a while, I doubted Quinn would ever forgive the man who was now her husband.

Would Ava forgive me once the truth finally came out? If she didn't, I had no idea how I'd feel. For the first time in my life, it mattered. Somewhere deep in the confines of my heart, it mattered a great deal.

16

Ava

I wanted to sleep, but my brain refused to cooperate. All night, I'd tossed and turned, thinking about Tabon.

When the sun came up, I went downstairs, made myself a cup of coffee, and sat by the window, watching the waves crash against the rocks below. It would be at least three or four hours before my sister, Pen, or Tara would get up. Maybe longer.

I padded into a room where I'd noticed bookshelves the night before. Maybe I could find something to read that would hold my attention enough that I wouldn't think about the man sleeping next door, and how much I wished I was in bed next to him.

I was perusing the vast collection of books when I heard the sound of a car. From where I stood, I could see it pull directly into the garage on the other side of the house.

I crept over to the window and peered through the draperies. A very beautiful woman came out of the garage, entered a code on the keypad to lower the door, and approached the entrance of Tabon's side.

I watched as the front door opened and the woman slipped inside.

How could I have been so stupid? I'd thought Tabon was truly interested in me, but the reality of what I'd just seen proved I'd been wrong. When I wouldn't sleep with him, he found someone who would.

I had to get out of here. There was no way I could spend another minute in this house. I raced upstairs to tell Aine that I was leaving. My sister and our two friends could stay as long as they wanted, but I was going home.

"Oh my God, Ava, what time is it?" Aine said when I shook her awake.

"I don't know…close to seven."

My sister rubbed her eyes and sat up in bed. "What's going on?"

"I have to leave."

"Wait. What?"

"Wake up, for Christ's sake. I said I'm leaving."

Aine's eyes opened wide. "Sit down and tell me what's going on."

I sat on the edge of the other twin bed in the room.

"I just saw a woman go in Tabon's front door."

"Now?"

I nodded. "I couldn't sleep, so I was looking for something to read. She pulled her car into the garage, closed the door, and then went inside the house. I couldn't see Tabon, but someone opened the door for her, and I didn't see Gunner's SUV parked where it had been last night."

"I'm so sorry, Ava," said Aine. "I really thought he liked you."

So had I, but obviously, the word had a loose definition. He may like me, but that didn't mean he wouldn't invite someone else into his bed.

"What are you going to do?"

"Catch a flight home as soon as I can."

"I think there's an airport in San Luis Obispo."

"I'll go see when the first flight out is, and then figure out how I'll get there."

"I can take you."

"That's okay. Go back to sleep."

"As if that's an option. I'll just pack up and go home with you."

"What about Penelope and Tara? I doubt they'll want to leave so soon. And if we take the car, how are they supposed to get around?"

"Good point. We could call a car service."

"You should stay," I told her.

"No. It's okay. Really."

"I'd rather you did."

"Oh."

"I'm humiliated and embarrassed, Aine. I just want to go home, and I'd rather be alone."

My sister nodded. "Let me know when your flight is, and we'll decide from there."

17

My phone pinged right as I was pulling into the driveway of the Harmony house. I opened the alert from the tracking device I'd planted in Ava's purse, and saw she was on the move.

"What's happening?" I barked at Alegria when she answered my call.

"The subject left by car ten minutes ago."

"By herself?"

No. A car service, sir."

"And you let her?"

I disconnected the call, watched Ava's progress, and called Gunner.

"Change of plans. Ava is on the move."

"Roger that. Does Alegria have her covered?"

"Yes, but an unknown driver picked her up at the house roughly fifteen minutes ago."

"I'm right behind you."

I continued to watch Ava's movements on the app, ready to pull onto the highway as soon as they sped by.

I looked in my rearview mirror and saw Gunner on Mercer's Ducati.

I'd been following the car Ava was in for twenty minutes. She appeared to be the sole occupant other than the driver. If I had to guess, I'd say she was on her way to the airport.

I called Doc. "See if Ava is booked on any flights out of SLO."

"Merrigan's thoughts as well when we saw she was on the move. She is, and it leaves for JFK in a little over an hour."

"Traveling alone?"

"Appears that way."

"Thank Fatale for me," I said before disconnecting the call.

Ava was sneaking home, by herself, without as much as a word to me. Why?

She'd seemed miffed when we went to the grocery store last night, but that didn't explain why she'd done such an about-face. One minute she was telling me she wanted to feel me pulsing inside her, the next she announced she wanted to go to bed alone.

I placed another call, this time to Aine McNamara.

"I'd ask how you got my number, but I suppose you can get that kind of information easily," she said.

"Why did your sister leave?"

"Getting right to the point."

"Yep. Help me out here, Aine. What the hell happened?"

I heard her snicker and mumble something unintelligible.

"What's that?"

"She saw a woman going into your place this morning."

I'd ask what she'd been doing up at that hour, but then I'd only sound guilty.

"She works for me."

"TMI, Razor."

"What's TMI?"

"Too much information."

"I know what it means. Why is a woman working for me TMI?"

"I'd rather not know the details of what she does for you."

Aine knew enough about K19 and the kind of work we did that I could be at least partially honest with her.

"She's an operative, working on assignment for our firm."

"Requiring her to arrive at dawn?"

"That's right."

"I doubt Ava will believe you."

I got the picture, but that didn't explain her sudden change last night.

"She really likes you, Razor. She told me she was embarrassed and humiliated."

"Understood."

"I'm asking you not to play with her. The persona she projects isn't who she really is."

"I hear you, Aine, and I have no intention of hurting her. I like her too."

I scrubbed my face with my hand after disconnecting the call, and thought hard about how I could convince Ava to come back to the house with me, without having to divulge that I was, in essence, her bodyguard. It would be hard enough to come up with a reason for how I knew she was about to board a flight home.

I really wished Quinn and Mercer hadn't left. At least Quinn understood the way the team worked, and might have been able to convince Ava to give me a shot.

Alegria and Gunner followed the car Ava was in to the terminal departure area while I pulled into the short term lot and parked.

I'll make contact, I messaged both of them.

I sprinted inside, hoping to catch Ava before she went through security.

When she approached near where I stood, I saw that she'd been crying. Did I really matter that much to her?

"Hi," I said, stepping out of the shadows.

Ava put her hand on her heart.

"I'm sorry I startled you."

"I guess I shouldn't be surprised to see you here."

I shook my head.

"Why, though?"

"Because I don't want you to leave."

"Try again," she said.

"What do you mean?"

"Tell me the truth, Razor. Why are you here?"

"That is the truth."

Ava turned to walk away.

"Wait," I said, putting my hand on her shoulder. "Would you consider sitting down with me for a minute?"

Ava looked at her phone. "For a minute."

I led her over to a bank of seats with no one sitting nearby. She sat and crossed her arms.

"First of all, the woman you saw going into my house this morning works for K19. She's an operative on assignment for us."

Ava nodded and I took a deep breath.

"You have a clear picture of how Quinn and Mercer met?"

She nodded a second time.

"Mercer was on assignment, protecting her."

"Yes. I'm aware of that, Razor."

"But he had feelings for her that had nothing to do with his assignment. He genuinely cared about her, and I'd go so far as to say he loved her, even in the beginning."

"My flight is boarding soon."

God, how could I put this in a way that wouldn't make it sound like my only interest in her was as an asset I needed to protect.

"The case against Dash Finnegan is more complex than anyone has led you to believe. You may think you're testifying solely against him; however, the feds and the CIA are more interested in bringing down the people he works for than the man himself."

"What are you saying?"

"I'm saying that I have been hired to protect you, Avarie."

I waited for her to process what I told her, watching in agony as her eyes filled with tears.

"It was all an act?"

"Never." I leaned forward and cupped her cheek with my palm. "What I feel for you is very real. I told you I couldn't stop thinking about you, but the truth is that I've spent the last year wanting to know what it would be like to kiss you, wanting to just be with you—that was all the truth, sweetheart."

"When did your assignment, or whatever you call it, start?"

"Yesterday."

"That's why you invited us to stay with you?"

"It is. However, that isn't all there is to it, Ava. I wanted you to stay with me. I *wanted* you, any way I could have you. I still do."

"What would you do if I got on my flight?"

"I'd go with you."

"Is the woman working with you to protect me?"

"Yes. As is Gunner."

"Who else knows about this?"

"Doc and Merrigan, and our contact at the agency."

"Do you know who Dash works for?"

I nodded, wishing she hadn't asked.

"You can't tell me, can you?"

"No. I can't."

I'd give anything to know what Ava was thinking, but I'd be patient and wait for her next move. Would she get on that plane? If she did, would I be able to get a ticket in time to take the same flight? If not, I'd have to put someone in New York on her detail until I arrived.

"I'm glad you were finally honest with me."

"There's something else I want you to know. I asked for this assignment, Ava. Gunner tried to talk me out of it. Doc did too."

"Why?"

"Because falling for your asset is dangerous, and for me, it was already too late. I fell for you long before I knew there was an assignment."

"If it's dangerous, why are you doing it?"

I leaned even closer. "Because I could never forgive myself if something happened to you, and there's no one else I trust enough to keep you as safe as I will."

Her eyes were fixated on mine, as though she was trying to reconcile what I was telling her.

"What are you going to do, Ava? Will you come back to the house with me, or will you get on the plane?"

"Is anyone else in danger because of me?"

"No."

"Not Aine?"

"Not to my knowledge."

"Have you had sex with the woman who came to your house this morning?"

That question was so far out of left field, I felt like she was administering a polygraph.

"I have not. What else do you want to know, Ava?"

She studied me, not giving me any indication of what she might say or do next. I knew her flight had to be boarding soon, but I refused to look away from her even to check the time.

"This can't be like Mercer and Quinn. I can't have a relationship with you, Razor. I know that means two different things to you and me. But for me, it means I cannot have sex with you."

I nodded, hating that since we started talking, she hadn't called me Tabon once.

"Here's the other thing. If you lie to me, I'm going to ask you to quit this…assignment, or whatever it is, and get someone else to take over."

"I can't make that promise, Ava."

"I see."

"I'm being as honest as I know how right now. You may have questions that I can't answer. Or won't answer. I'll lie to keep you safe, Ava. I'll do anything to keep you safe."

"Couldn't you just be honest instead? If you can't tell me something, just say so."

"I can say, here and now, that I can, but if it comes down to your safety, and I feel I have no choice but to keep the truth from you, that's what I'll do."

"What about the other thing I said?"

That was more difficult for me to talk about. In my heart, I hoped she didn't mean it. But if she wanted honesty, I'd give it to her.

"I want you to listen to me, Avarie."

She nodded.

"I'm crazy about you. There are times I feel like I want you more than I want to breathe. The truth is, I hope you change your mind. In the meantime, though, I want you to stay with me, not in Gunner's side of the house, in mine. That doesn't mean we have to share a bed; it just means that now that you know the true nature of what is happening, having you that close will make it a lot easier for me to do my job."

"Anything else?" she asked.

"Yeah. I don't want you to call me Razor. My name is Tabon."

"That's your father's name."

"True, but just like you are insisting on my being honest, I'm insisting you call me Tabon."

"Okay," she said softly.

"Ready to go back to the house?" I asked.

"I checked my bag."

"Gunner intercepted it."

"He's here?"

"Yep."

"Is the woman here?"

"She is, Ava. She's helping to protect you."

"I don't want her to."

I scrubbed my hand over my face. "Can I ask why not?"

"Because I don't."

"We can talk about it, okay?"

"It's a deal breaker, Tabon."

"If you feel that strongly, I can have her reassigned."

"I do."

18

Ava

If Tabon had asked again why I was insisting the woman, whatever her name was, not be part of the group of people protecting me, I wasn't sure I could be as honest as I was asking him to be.

Plain and simple, I was jealous. The woman I'd seen this morning was ridiculously beautiful and, if they were colleagues, far better suited for him than I was.

Thankfully, he hadn't asked, so I didn't have to lie.

"I'm in short-term parking," he said as we walked out of the airport.

I nodded, hating how unsure of myself I felt. This wasn't normal for me. No matter how insecure I felt on the inside, I'd always been able to project nothing but confidence. Aine had asked me about it so many times when we were growing up. How I did it, and also, why she hadn't gotten that personality trait?

I couldn't say. All I knew was that, right now, I didn't have it either. When I was with Tabon, I questioned myself in a way I never had before.

It was a good thing I'd told him I wouldn't have sex with him. The anxiety I would've felt about whether I was good enough for him, would have ruined it for me anyway.

"What about Aine?" I asked.

"It would be better if she wasn't aware of the situation."

"Which means I have to lie to her." I sighed. Maybe I was beginning to understand how hard it would be for someone in Tabon's position to be completely honest.

He stopped walking, so I did too.

"There isn't anything about this that's easy, Ava. I wish there was a way for you to talk to Quinn, because she could give you some insight like only a person who has been in your position would be able to do. It was much harder for Quinn's mother."

"Lena?"

Tabon nodded. "She never had a normal life, not since she was younger than you are now."

"How did she die?"

I watched as Tabon closed his eyes and took a deep breath. "I can't tell you that, Ava."

"I understand."

He walked a few feet farther and stopped again. "This is me," he said pointing to a dark-gray Porsche Cayenne. The liftgate opened, he put my bag in the back, and then opened the passenger door.

We were a few minutes into the drive when a call came through from Doc. I knew because his name appeared on the screen built into the dash. Tabon didn't answer.

"It's not the kind of conversation I want to have while I'm driving," he explained.

"Are there things you're afraid he'll say that you don't want me to hear?"

"Yes."

"Is this hard for you?"

Tabon laughed out loud. "You have no idea. Mainly, I don't want you to hear his reaction when I tell him everything I've told you. As I said before, he was against me taking this assignment."

Hearing that for the second time hurt worse than the first. "Am I really that bad?"

Tabon reached over and grasped my hand. "The opposite, actually. He knows I have feelings for you, Ava. The other thing he objected to was my initiating a relationship with you as a way to be close enough to protect you. That bothered him a lot more."

"So, how does this work?"

"I'm glad you asked, because we need to set some ground rules."

I didn't like the direction this conversation was headed. Rules had never been my strong suit. I'd spent far too much time in the headmistress' office because rules, as far as I was concerned, were meant to be broken. I looked over at Tabon, who was grinning.

"Do you think this is funny?" I asked.

"Not at all. You just let me know in about the clearest way possible what you think of rules."

"I did?"

"Oh, yeah."

"Let's get this over with. What are they?"

"Your cell phone needs to go, along with credit and debit cards. We'll have to negotiate who knows where you are and how much they know."

"Negotiate?"

"My position is that no one knows anything. I can't imagine you'll be okay with that."

"I have to tell Aine something, and I'd prefer to tell her as much of the truth as I can."

"Anyone else?"

"As long as I don't have to be the one to tell them, I guess it's okay if Pen and Tara think I've gone MIA because you and I can't keep our hands off each other."

"I wouldn't mind turning that into the truth."

"Tabon…"

"Can't have it both ways, Avarie. Either I'm honest or I'm not."

It was my pride that made me issue the edict that I couldn't, or wouldn't, have sex with him. While my brain knew it was for the best when I said it, and even knew it now, just being next to him in the car was a struggle to keep my mind off how amazing he'd look naked.

He brought my hand to his mouth and kissed the back of it. "I'm not going to lie or pretend that I don't want you."

"But…"

"Go ahead. Say whatever is on your mind."

"What happens if we do, and then you don't want to again?"

"I'm going to fill in some of your blanks. What happens if we have sex, and then I don't want to have sex with you again?"

I nodded.

"Tell you what. Let's wait until we get back to the house to finish this conversation."

That was fine with me. Never would be okay too.

"We need to finish the other conversation now, though."

"Rules?"

Tabon nodded. "You didn't object to not using your cell phone or credit cards."

"How will I pay for anything?"

"You won't."

"What if—"

"Whatever you need, I'll take care of."

Never in my life had I been put on a budget, especially one so austere. However, I could handle it. It would probably be good for me to go without for once in my life.

"Good with getting rid of your cell phone?"

"I can't talk to anyone anyway, so I don't know what difference it makes."

"Hand it over, then."

I did and watched as he took it apart.

"Was that necessary?"

"Yep. We'll do a sweep of your belongings when we get back to the house too."

"Why?"

"Because someone could be tracking you."

"Were you tracking me?"

It was one of those questions Tabon struggled to answer. I was beginning to pick up on more of his tells.

"Yes," he finally said.

"It's okay, Tabon. I understand."

"I'm glad you do. Last question, then. What about your parents?"

I looked away, willing my eyes not to tear up. No matter how I responded, I was going to sound like I felt sorry for myself, and to a certain extent, I did.

I loved my parents. My mom was far more trying than my dad, but neither had been very parental. Aine and I weren't certain our mother's pregnancy had been accidental, but there were times when we both felt like a big inconvenience.

"We aren't close," I answered.

"Your father wanted to have dinner when you returned to New York."

"He won't remember saying he did."

"Ava, look at me."

I shook my head. The tears I tried to will away were threatening to spill over on my cheeks, and that was the last thing I wanted Tabon to see.

"Please, baby. Look at me."

I brushed away my tears and turned my head.

"Let me take care of you."

I wasn't sure exactly what he meant, but right now, having someone like him take care of me, no matter how, sounded so good. How nice would it be to not have to be in charge of my own life, even for a little while. I had been since I was seven years old.

Aine and I had never had to worry about money, and thankfully, we'd both been responsible with it. Neither of us got in trouble with drugs or hung out with the wrong crowd. Neither of us were what I would consider extravagant either. From time to time, our father would ask if the amount of our monthly stipend was adequate. It had always been more than enough, given he paid for our apartment and the associated expenses, along with school.

But being taken care of didn't relate solely to money. Sometimes I just wanted to put my head on someone's shoulder and let them make the world go away, even for a short amount of time.

Dash had never done that for me. If anything, I was the more responsible person in our relationship. When I last saw him, and witnessed the meeting I wished I never had, I'd guessed that he was going to try to get back together with me, given I heard his wedding had been called off.

He'd looked terrible too. He was thinner than I'd ever known him to be, and he looked exhausted. I told myself that his criminal activities were certainly to blame, but if he'd gotten mixed up in something bigger, maybe the way he looked was a result of the pressure he was under.

"Where did you go?"

I turned and looked at Tabon. "Just thinking about Dash and what a mess he made of his life."

"I'm sorry you had to get involved."

"Me too."

"Hungry?"

"I'd say no, but the last time you asked, I ate twice as much as you did."

19

Razor

I turned off the highway onto Moonstone Beach Drive and pulled off to park on the ocean side.

"This is one of my favorite breakfast spots," I told her, pointing to the Ollalieberry Diner.

"It smells delicious."

"The muffins are big enough to share," I said and then laughed when she looked skeptical.

Before we crossed the road, I took her hand in mine, and when we reached the other side, I put my arm around her shoulders.

"Is this part of my protection?" she asked.

"Me having my hands on you? Not at all." If she'd let me, I'd never let her be far enough away that I couldn't touch her.

While it had been painful to see how sad her relationship with her parents made her, that she didn't ask if she could contact them, was a relief.

We ended up sharing two muffins, one ollalieberry and one peach; Ava ordered an omelet, and I had eggs and bacon.

"I need to go for a run this afternoon," she said, rubbing her stomach.

"Me too, and then spend a couple of hours in the gym."

"Is there one in town?"

"There's one in the house."

"Oh. That's convenient. Where do you run?"

"When I'm here or home, I prefer the beach."

"Where's home?"

"Ever heard of Yachats?"

"Nope."

"It's on the Oregon Coast." I was still trying to figure out a way to get her there. "I'd love for you to see it."

I waited for her to say something, anything really, but she was acting like she hadn't heard me.

"Ava?"

"Do you take all the women you protect there?" she whispered.

"I've never taken anyone there. Not even Gunner," I whispered back.

As close as we were, I couldn't help myself. I leaned forward and kissed her.

"Mmm," I said, licking my lips. "You taste like peaches. I like it."

I kissed her again, anticipating that she might pull away from me, but she didn't, and nothing could've made me happier.

"Ready?" I said when the waitress returned with my credit card and receipt.

"Sure."

"When we get back, I'm taking your bag straight to my place."

"I don't have much with me."

"We can always go into town and pick up whatever you need."

She raised an eyebrow.

"What?"

"I don't have any money, Tabon. At least not that I can use."

We were standing next to my car, and I trapped her between it and my body. "I told you to let me take care of you, Avarie."

"I don't think that includes buying me clothes."

"It includes everything you need, clothes too."

I lowered my head and kissed her again, praying she wouldn't stop me, and she didn't. No matter what she told herself, Ava wanted me as much as I wanted her. If we were having this much trouble keeping our hands off each other after only a few hours, how would it be between us after a few days?

20

"He talked me into staying," I told Aine when we got back to the house.

"He came to the airport?" Penelope gasped from just outside the bedroom door.

I looked at Aine, who shrugged.

"I had to tell them you left."

"It's like a movie. Did he call your name over the pager system and profess his undying love?" asked Pen.

"Hardly, but he did ask me to stay in a very convincing way."

"Is that why your suitcase appears to be missing?"

"There's no point in pretense, Pen. I'm going to be staying on the other side of the duplex with him."

"Does this mean you won't be joining us for wine tasting again today?"

I shook my head. "I think we may go for a run."

"Oh my God. Can you imagine running with that hard body?"

"Yeah. I sure can." I looked over at Aine, who wasn't laughing.

"Can you give us a minute, Pen?"

"Of course," she said, closing the bedroom door behind her.

Aine got right to the point. "What's going on?"

"You can't tell a single soul."

My sister nodded. "Okay."

"I saw something I shouldn't have. Involving Dash. It's pretty bad, and he's been arrested."

"You're kidding?" Aine gasped.

"I have to testify against him."

Aine turned white. "Is Tabon like…your bodyguard?"

I put my finger in front of my lips. "You can't tell a soul. Not even Mom and Dad."

"I won't, I promise."

"I wasn't supposed to tell you as much as I have."

"You know you can trust me."

"It isn't that. The more you know…you could be in danger too."

Aine nodded, but I doubted she had any idea how serious the situation was.

"There's something else. On our way back from the airport and then again after breakfast, Tabon said he wanted to take care of me."

Aine put her hand on her heart. "He cares about you. He called me."

"When?"

"After you left. I told him about you seeing the woman going into his house."

I heard a knock and expected to see Pen or Tara when I told whoever it was to come in. Instead, it was Tabon, who came in and closed the door behind him.

"Here," he said, handing a phone to Aine. "Ava will be able to call you, but you won't be able to return calls to her. If anyone gets their hands on this phone, there will be no link to your sister."

Tabon handed me a phone as well. "You'll get a new one at least every few days, unless I see a reason for it to be more often."

"Thank you."

"This is unorthodox, but it is the only solution I could come up with for you to be able to stay in touch. Aine, if you have any concerns, if you haven't heard from Ava in a few days, you can contact Doc directly." He handed her a card. "Memorize this number."

She nodded, murmuring her thanks as well.

"You and your two friends will be leaving in under two hours—"

"Why?" I asked.

"They'll be having a lot of fun, I promise."

"Oh, I love San Francisco," Aine said, opening the envelope he handed to her.

"Gunner will drive you to the airport and make sure you have everything you need. He's briefing Penelope and Tara now."

"I'm going to miss you so much," I said, standing to hug my sister.

"I'll be downstairs," he said, walking out the door and closing it behind him.

"Briefing?" said Aine, laughing.

"He speaks a different language sometimes."

My sister pulled me down to sit next to her on the bed. "You really like him," she said.

"I do, but…it's complicated."

"We wish you would come with us," said Penelope when I came downstairs behind Aine. "But we understand that you have your own plans."

"You take good care of her," said Tara, punching Tabon's arm. Yes, he would, I thought, but not in the way Tara was thinking. Actually, maybe he would in the way she was thinking as well.

"Ready?" he asked after I hugged my two friends and my sister one more time.

"See you soon, and have an amazing time," I said, taking Tabon's outstretched hand.

"I'm proud of you," he said when we walked in his front door.

"I hate lying."

Tabon stood in front of me, with his hands on my shoulders. "You didn't."

"I feel like I did."

"Let's go run it out of your system."

21

Razor

When we got to the mile mark, I asked Ava if she was ready to turn back.

"Only if you are," she said and then kept going without waiting for me to respond.

At the next mile mark, I asked again if she wanted to head back, and again she said she didn't.

"How far do you usually run?" I asked.

"Between ten and eleven miles, typically. But when I'm training, I'll do a long run every week or ten days."

"Marathon runner, eh?"

"It's my stress relief."

"I hear ya."

I didn't ask about turning around again until we hit the five-mile mark, and by then, she was willing.

"Taking pity on me?" I asked.

"Why do I think you could outrun me any day of the week?"

When we got back to the house, I collapsed on a deck chair while Ava stretched.

"I need water. Can I get you some?" she asked.

"I can get it."

Before I could stand, she pushed me back into the chair. "Rest, old man."

"We're back to that now, are we?"

I shook my head when she went inside. Had it ever been so easy with any other woman? I hadn't had a long-term relationship pretty much ever. The last I could remember was in high school.

It wasn't just that Ava was beautiful, or that her body brought me to my knees, she was funny and smart, and definitely outpaced me on our run.

"What's next?" she asked, setting my water in front of me.

"Come here."

"I am here."

"Closer," I said, catching her arm. "Right here." I pointed to my lap.

"Tabon…I'm all sweaty."

"So am I." I pulled her down and nuzzled her neck. "Do you have any idea how unbelievably sexy your ass is in those shorts? For ten whole miles, you and those shorts tortured me."

"How can I make it up to you?"

"That is a very open-ended question, Avarie."

She smiled.

"It hasn't been that many hours since you told me you couldn't have sex with me."

"I told you before I change my mind a lot."

I pulled back and looked into her eyes. "I want you out of those shorts."

When Ava got off my lap, I expected her to lecture me, or turn me down, or ignore me. Instead, she took my hand.

"Let's go inside," she murmured, her voice husky with desire.

I picked her up instead. "Put your legs around me, baby."

When she did, I tilted my head, angling to claim her mouth.

"Tabon—" She sighed.

My mouth slammed into hers when she flattened her palms against my chest. Instead of pushing for me to let her go, she fisted my shirt, keeping me as close to her as she could.

Her whimpers and mewls would be my undoing. As much as I wanted to take it slow, I couldn't. I thrust my tongue past her lips, inhaling her passion as she kissed me back.

Holding her tight, I climbed the stairs with her in my arms. I kicked open the bedroom door, laid her on the bed, and settled by her side.

"Tabon," she said for the second time.

"Talk to me, Ava. Tell me what you need, what you want."

"I don't want you to have so many clothes on."

"Not a problem." I stood.

"Let me," she said, rolling off the bed to stand in front of me.

I didn't remember a woman ever undressing me while she remained fully clothed, but I was happy to let Ava be the first—and the last if I had my way.

She pulled my t-shirt up and over my head. Her hands rested on the waistband of my shorts, and her eyes met mine.

"Go ahead, baby. I'll never stop you from putting your hands on me."

She pulled down my shorts and got to her knees. I could feel her heated breath as her fingers wrapped around my cock. When her tongue darted out and I felt the wetness of it, I almost came right then.

"I want you too bad, Ava. I need you as naked as I am."

She groaned but stood when I pulled her to her feet.

"I'm so sweaty," she said.

"We've already established that I like you that way."

"I like you that way too."

I pulled her shirt over her head as she'd done with mine and then knelt in front of her, pulling down her shorts and panties. When I leaned forward to kiss her pussy, Ava's hands gripped my hair.

"That's not fair," she moaned.

"I never promised to be fair," I said, spreading her legs and licking. "I want you open for me, baby."

I only hesitated long enough to look in her eyes. When I saw the same amount of desire that I had for her, I tore my gaze from hers and feasted my eyes on the slick flesh between her legs.

"Do you want my mouth on you, Ava?"

She shook her head. "I want you inside me, Tabon," she whimpered.

I licked her gently, groaning when her fingers twined again in my hair as I leisurely teased her with the tip of my tongue.

"Come for me, baby," I told her. "Don't hold anything back from me."

"I can't…I need you…"

I accepted the challenge she didn't know she'd given me, working her into a frenzy as I licked, laved, and sucked her flesh. My fingers fondled the swollen button of nerves at the top of her sex, and knew that, within seconds, she'd have no choice but to let go of her inhibitions and come all over my tongue.

"Scream for me, baby," I urged. "Let me hear how much you love what I'm doing to you."

Ava didn't disappoint as she fell apart under the insistence of my mouth and hands. She rocked against me as she slowly came back down from the heights of pleasure. I released her, and she fell back on the bed.

"God…Tabon…I never…"

Before she could say any more, I sheathed myself in a condom and thrust into her tightness. I stopped and waited for her body to get accustomed to my girth.

"Tabon, I need more," she groaned, holding the cheeks of my ass in her hands and forcing me deeper.

Her fingernails dug in as I felt her tighten around me. "I'm…oh God…I'm…"

"Go ahead, Ava. Let go. Let me feel you come on me."

She clamped down, and yet, I wasn't ready for this to end. As her body relaxed, I slowed my thrusts, driving into her.

"Look at me," I demanded. "I want you to see the same pleasure on my face as I saw on yours."

When her glassy eyes met mine, I let myself go.

"I could spend the rest of my life just like this," I murmured as I rested beside her, "with you naked next to me."

"Tabon, that was…"

"Yeah?"

"Mind-blowing."

I rolled her to her side, so her back was to my front. I nestled my cock between the cheeks of her ass and started slowly moving against her. I reached around and pinched the nipples I'd yet to get my mouth on.

Ava moaned, pressed back against me, and covered my hands with hers.

"Mmm, I think you like this," I murmured, nipping at the soft skin on her neck. "You're so responsive, Ava, so damn gorgeous as you give yourself to me."

I moved one hand away from her breast, and she moaned. I smiled and reached for another condom.

"I want you on your hands and knees, baby."

When she rolled and did as I asked, I twined my fingers in her hair and thrust into her with no hesitation. Her back arched as I held her in place so I could pound into her heat with my own rhythm.

Once again I roared my release, and when I did, I felt her shudder and come right along with me.

I let her roll to her back, and then raised my head to feast on her breasts. When my tongue toyed with her nipple, Ava squirmed.

"Sensitive?" I asked, grinning.

"Yes," she answered trying to cover her nipples with her hands.

"Uh, no." I grasped her wrists and held them in place while my tongue laved each nipple, going back and forth between the two.

I could do this for hours, sleep, and then do it all again. I wanted her in every way she'd let me have her, and I wanted it right now. What had she said? What if

I had her and didn't want her again? That was impossible. I knew I'd never get my fill of Ava McNamara.

She'd gone to start the shower, and soon, I'd join her. First, I needed to check in with Gunner to make sure he'd taken Alegria off the assignment.

"Hey, man," I said when Gunner answered.

"Everything is taken care of," he snapped.

"What's up?"

"There's been some chatter. I think we were too sloppy when we took the girls to the house."

"Do we need to change location?"

"I'd say the sooner you can, the better."

"I want to take her to Yachats. Should we fly commercial?"

"Fuck, no."

"What else is goin' on?"

"Nothin'."

I wouldn't push, but I'd known Gunner Godet for too many years to not know when he was lying.

"Who's comin' along?"

"Me and Monk for now."

"Roger that," I said. "I'll be back in touch in a few."

"We'll meet you at the airfield."

I disconnected the call and went into the bathroom where Ava was showering. I could see the lines of her drop-dead-gorgeous body through the steamy glass and started to harden all over again.

Her eyes were closed as she wound shampoo through her long hair, and her body glistened where the water spread the lather.

"God, woman," I growled, opening the door and joining her. I ran my hands over her slick skin, groaning again, knowing we didn't have time to continue what we'd started earlier.

"Are you sore?" I asked. "I wasn't exactly gentle."

"A little," she answered, her cheeks flushing under my intent gaze.

"Let me take care of you, baby," I said, taking the soap from her hand and running it all over her body.

"I love the way you say that, Tabon," she murmured, opening her eyes to gauge my reaction.

"I love the way you say my name. Especially when I'm buried deep inside you."

I looked up at the ceiling, reminding myself again we didn't have time for me to love on her body the way I wanted to.

I washed the soap from her neck and shoulders and then kissed each one, running my tongue up to just below her ear.

"We need to leave soon," I murmured.

"Where are we going?" she asked with her eyes still closed, concentrating on the feel of my hands and lips.

"I'm taking you home with me."

"When?"

"As soon as we're done in here. We'll pack and then leave."

"I don't think I ever unpacked."

I smiled. "We need to get you some more clothes, baby."

"Why?"

Yeah. Why? I'd be perfectly happy having her naked twenty-four seven.

22

Ava

"Whose plane is that?" I asked when I looked out the window of the airfield's terminal and saw a Bombardier.

"K19's."

My father had his own plane, but it was nowhere near as big as the one we were about to board.

Tabon motioned for me to go ahead of him.

"This is Onyx," he said when the pilot greeted us at the end of the jetway. "And that's Alegria." He pointed to the woman about to go into the cockpit.

"We'll be in the air a little over two hours," Onyx said before going into the cockpit himself.

"Tabon, why—"

"She's one of our pilots. She's no longer on your detail, but we need her to co-pilot on this flight."

I nodded, wishing I'd never have to see that woman again.

"Have a seat, baby." He pointed to several chairs in what looked more like a luxurious living room than the inside of an aircraft.

"We usually have a flight attendant, but I didn't think it was necessary for such a short trip."

"Will you tell me where we're going?"

"We're flying into Eugene, and then we'll drive to the coast."

"Yachats?" I asked.

He nodded and smiled, making my mouth water.

The first time I saw him, he'd been in board shorts and a t-shirt. Him in a tuxedo at the wedding had almost brought me to my knees. Today he wore a pair of jeans that showed off not just his ass but the bulge in the front too. I couldn't let my gaze linger there too long, though. I already yearned to be with him again, and it hadn't been much more than an hour since he'd had his hands on my naked body.

The first two buttons of the burnt-orange Henley shirt that strained taut across his muscular chest were unfastened, and his black motorcycle boots looked well used, but cared for at the same time.

Tabon exuded a power and confidence that made me want to walk into his arms and beg him to wake me up from the bad dream my life had recently become.

"Have a seat," he said for the second time, obviously waiting for me to choose first. When I did, he sat beside me.

"Gunner should be here soon." He looked at his phone. "I expected him to be here before we were."

"He was," said Onyx from the cockpit. "He asked me to tell you that he and Monk would be right back. Sorry, sir, it slipped my mind."

Tabon nodded, but didn't answer. He seemed distracted.

"Everything okay?" I asked.

He looked up from his phone. "We may need to rethink protection for your sister and your friends."

"Why?"

He hesitated, as though he was struggling with what he could tell me.

"We shouldn't have brought you to the duplex. None of you. That was my mistake."

"Are you saying someone knew we were there?"

"Not necessarily, but from now on, I need to be more careful."

I leaned over and rested my head on his shoulder.

"You're too hard on yourself," I murmured.

"How do you know the right words to make me feel better?"

Did I? How was it that I could read his expressions after spending so little time with him?

"After we land, we'll stop and get you some warmer clothes. If there's anything else you need, that will be the time to get it."

"What is your fixation with buying me clothes?"

He smiled. "You don't have anything suitable for where we'll be staying."

"There's a dress code?"

Tabon laughed. "It'll be colder than you expect."

"You could keep me warm."

"I plan to. You'll still need long pants, warmer shirts, and at least one jacket."

"I thought we were going to Oregon, not the Arctic."

Gunner came aboard with someone I hadn't met.

"Hello, sir," said the man.

"Monk, meet Ava McNamara," said Tabon.

The man shook my hand and sat next to Gunner in seats across from us. Gunner looked at me and then back at Tabon.

I got the hint and stood to move.

"Where are you going?"

"I thought I'd sit over there," I answered, pointing to another place. "That way you can talk, or whatever."

"I'll talk, or whatever, with you next to me."

"Raze…" said Gunner, but Tabon ignored him. Instead of answering, he ran his hand down my arm and intertwined his fingers with mine.

23

Razor

"We'll talk later," I said to Gunner, motioning for the two men to change seats.

"Try to sleep, Avarie," I whispered once they'd moved. "You'll need your rest."

I knew as soon as she had. First, her breathing evened out, and then she rested her head on my shoulder. I shifted so I could put my arm around her, and then reclined both our seats as far as they would go. A few minutes later, snoring softly, she put her arm around my waist. Only then did I allow myself to drift off too.

I opened my eyes when I felt the plane begin its descent, and rested my head against the top of Ava's. She felt so good in my arms.

My body came alive with the realization that the woman of my fantasies was once again snuggled against me. I shifted a little, which only made things worse when her hand moved from my waist down to my hips and I could feel her breasts against my chest.

When her forearm moved against the now-straining zipper of my jeans and she softly moaned, I almost jumped out of the seat. It was that or strip us both naked and make whatever she was dreaming about a reality. Instead, I moved her arm away from my body and turned so I could run my fingers down the side of her face.

I wanted to continue my exploration by trailing my fingertips from her cheek, down her neck to where her thin t-shirt was stretched tight over the lace of her bra, but I couldn't. Not with an audience, and not until I had all the time in the world to enjoy it.

"Time to wake up," I said softly.

"Tabon?" she said, sitting up. "Where are we?"

"About to land." I pulled her close to me and kissed her forehead. "We have five more minutes. Give it to me, Avarie."

"Give you what?"

"You, in my arms."

"Five more minutes," she whispered.

Five turned into twenty, which was how long it took them to land and taxi to the terminal.

"We're here," I said when I felt the plane come to a stop and Onyx power down the engine.

Her cheeks flushed, and she sat up, unfastening her own seatbelt and looking to see if Gunner or Monk were nearby.

"They moved to the front," I told her, smiling at her modesty.

"A car was delivered and is parked outside the hangar. Your luggage will be there shortly."

"Thanks, Alegria," I said as Ava and I deboarded.

"We'll be in touch," she added.

"Message me your twenty when you and Onyx get situated."

"Roger that, sir," she said, making eye contact with Ava, who was waiting for me just outside the plane on the jetway.

"Are they staying?" Ava asked as we walked through the small terminal.

"No. I just need to know where the plane is."

"So…you said she's a pilot."

"One of three we employ. Also a former operative, but soon to be a K19 partner."

"She has a French accent. Was she a spy?"

I nodded. She still was.

"Is that her real name?"

"No. It's Manon Mondreau."

"Wow. That's her name? Sounds like a sexy jazz singer."

I smiled.

"So you two never…"

"Had sex? No. I told you that before."

Ava nodded.

"Why do you ask?"

"The way she looked at you."

"She's a colleague, nothing more."

"Does she know that?"

"I don't understand."

"Are colleagues off-limits?"

Not necessarily, but I'd never noticed Alegria express an interest in me.

"Yes," I answered instead.

"You might want to tell her that before you make her a partner."

"Is this the only kind of car you drive?" Ava asked when the golf cart delivered us to the hangar and she saw another Porsche Cayenne parked outside.

I laughed. "Coincidence."

"Hmm," she murmured. I got the feeling she didn't buy it.

"Hungry?" I asked after we left the airfield and were on the highway.

"What time is it?"

"Four." We hadn't eaten since breakfast; she had to be as ravenous as I was.

"Um…"

I smiled, waiting for her to continue.

"Where's Gunner and the other guy?"

"They went ahead."

"Oh. Are they staying at your house too?"

"No, but they'll be nearby. Answer my question, baby. Are you hungry?"

"You can pretty much assume the answer to that question will always be yes."

Another thing I was crazy about. She had an appetite and wasn't afraid to eat when she was with me. So far, more than I did.

I loved her curves and softness, particularly now that I knew how it felt to sink deep inside her.

"There's a place I haven't been to in a couple of years, but it's been around forever, so I assume it's still good."

She smiled. "I'm pretty easy to please when it comes to food, Tabon."

I pulled off the highway and took a side road up a hill. "The view is spectacular from here."

Sweetwater was a restaurant I visited often with my grandmother. It had been one of her favorites, and I hadn't set foot in it since she passed away.

I parked and walked around to open Ava's door, thinking how I never imagined eating here again, and yet, now, it was important to me to share it with her.

"It's spectacular," she gasped, looking out at the three-hundred-and-sixty-degree view of rolling hills and vineyards.

"I thought you might like it."

I kept my hand on the small of her back as we walked along the garden pathway to the entrance.

"Did you talk to Gunner and the other guy?" Ava asked after we ordered.

I took a sip of my beer and nodded.

"Can you tell me anything?"

"No."

Ava wasn't happy with my response, but it was the truth; telling her what Gunner had come up with for her sister and friends would be giving her information there was no reason for her to know.

"Ava…"

"Look, I get it, okay? That doesn't mean I like it. Are they in danger because of me?"

"The whole idea is to keep them out of danger."

Ava's eyes filled with tears, and I covered her hand with mine.

"It's just that I can't believe all this is happening because I accidentally stumbled on a meeting that Dash was having with some thug."

I'd read the report and knew what Ava had seen and overheard, and she'd more than stumbled on a meeting. She'd witnessed Dash handing over sensitive information along with him receiving the payoff for it. If the "thug," as she'd called him, had realized she was witnessing the handoff, she'd be dead. That Dash didn't kill her meant one of two things. Either he didn't have the balls, or he still cared about her.

"I'm not the one who called in the anonymous tip either."

That, I'd known too.

When our food arrived, Ava took a few bites and pushed the rest around her plate.

"I thought you were always hungry," I said, trying to tease her into a better mood.

"I'm sorry."

I signaled the waiter, then asked for the check and for our food to be packaged to go.

"Let's go," I said when he returned with a to-go bag. "We need to pick up a few things in town before we head to the coast."

"I'm sure I'll be fine."

"Actually, you won't. There are four stores in Yachats, and not a single one sells women's clothing."

"I really don't feel like shopping."

"You don't have to."

She raised an eyebrow, and I thought maybe I saw a hint of a smile.

24

Ava

At the first store, Tabon picked out two pairs of jeans and a sweatshirt.

"These work," I said, coming out of the dressing room to find him waiting for me.

"Try these too." He exchanged what I had in my arms for what he had in his.

"I don't need—"

I turned around and went back into the dressing room when he leveled a mock glare at me.

"These are fine too," I said, opening the dressing room door, but Tabon wasn't there. I saw him at the cash register, handing the woman a credit card.

"These too." He took the clothes out of my hands when I approached.

"It's too much money. Please. I don't need all this."

"Don't worry about it."

"Right." Add feeling stupid to the already ever-present gut-wrenching guilt that had landed squarely on my chest, making it hard for me to breathe.

Had he really just told me not to worry about it? My life wasn't my own, and I had no idea when it would be again. I was completely dependent on him, and now, didn't even have the solace of talking to my sister.

What if he got tired of having me around, and sick of paying for everything? Then what would happen to me?

I had no "out." There hadn't been a time in my life when I didn't know that no matter what happened, I had my sister and our three best friends, who would do anything in their power to help me. If worse came to worst, I also had my parents. Not that I could imagine ever turning to them, but still.

No matter how nice Tabon was being right now, and even how hard he was trying to take care of me, I felt trapped. I turned away so he didn't see the tears that filled my eyes.

"Restroom?" I managed to eek out, hurrying in the direction the woman behind the counter pointed, and making it just in time before what little I ate came flying out.

I flushed the toilet and heard the door open, but didn't care who came in. I took deep breaths, my hands on my knees, as tears ran down my cheeks. I felt Tabon's hand on my back as he tried to soothe me.

"Come here." He pulled me into his arms.

"You shouldn't be in here," I said when another woman opened the door and glared at us.

"The only thing I shouldn't have done was leave the door unlocked." He took my hand and pulled me out of the ladies' room. "Come on, let's go."

Still holding my hand, he led me out the front door and across the street, to a park. He sat on a bench under a big oak tree and pulled me onto his lap.

"Talk to me, Avarie."

I shook my head.

"Please, tell me what's going on."

"You'll think I'm ungrateful, and I'm not. I appreciate everything you and Gunner and everyone else is doing to keep me safe."

"But something is bothering you enough that you were sick to your stomach."

How could I put into words that relying on him terrified me? It wasn't just that I didn't know what I'd do if he decided he didn't want to anymore; there was far more to it now.

What would he say if I told him I couldn't bear the idea of him not wanting *me* anymore, or that I'd be heartbroken if that happened? We'd had a morning of crazy, amazing sex. That's it. His heart wasn't invested in me like mine was in him, and it probably never would be.

"I know this is hard for you," he began. "I also know what your life has been like up to this point."

"You do?"

Tabon nodded. "For every smile, there were ten tears, twenty moments of sadness, and even more fear and uncertainty."

How had he jumped right over all the superficial things I was feeling and straight into the deepest, darkest of my fears? I'd always been afraid of being alone, because other than Aine, I had no one. Without my sister, I was lost. Aine grounded me and kept me from letting my emotions spin out of control. My parents had never filled that role in my life.

He stroked the side of my face with his fingertip.

"Don't hide your feelings from me, Avarie. I understand them better than most, and I'm always willing to let you talk through them, or just hold you. Whatever you need."

"My sister and I have never been apart," I murmured. "I mean there were times when we were, but there's never been a time when I couldn't talk to Aine if I wanted to, and vice versa."

"I know that, which is why I made arrangements for you to be able to."

"But…"

"Did you think that because we were making arrangements to send them away for a few days, you wouldn't be able to talk to her?"

I nodded.

"All you had to do was ask me," he said, wiping my tears away. "There was no reason for you to get this upset."

I took a couple of deep breaths and looked up at the leaves rustling on the limbs of the tree.

"Better?" he asked.

"Yeah, I think so."

"We have a couple more stops to make."

"What for?"

"Shoes, socks, that kind of stuff."

"Do I really need all that?"

"Are you hiking with me in those?" he asked, pointing to my sandals.

At every store, Tabon picked out twice what I thought I'd need.

"I can carry some of those." I pointed to the bags he was lugging with him.

"Here's the car." He set the bags on the sidewalk and clicked the fob to open the back hatch.

I walked over to the passenger door and waited for him to open it.

"We aren't finished," he said.

"What else could I possibly need?"

He didn't answer, but took my hand and pulled me into the next store.

"Oh. I don't need any of…this."

"Sure you do. I don't like doing laundry."

He walked straight over to a table that held all sorts of bra and panty sets, picking out several in my exact size.

"I don't want to think about how you know my bra size," I said.

He looked down at my breasts. "Am I wrong?"

I felt my cheeks heat and swatted him. "No. *Oh my God.*"

He handed what he'd chosen to the waiting sales-clerk and walked over to the nightie section.

"What's your favorite color?" he asked.

"Dark blue."

"Hmm." He ran his hands over the silky lingerie and picked out a couple, one pale pink, the other seafoam green. "These are my favorites," he whispered before asking the saleswoman if she had anything in the color I'd told him.

"Would you like a fitting room?" she asked once Tabon had added several other items to the woman's already heavily laden arms.

"They'll fit," he answered, motioning in the direction of the checkout area.

When I heard the total of the purchases from this store alone, I did some quick mental math. Tabon had spent over two thousand dollars in the course of the last hour.

I put my hand on his arm. "I'll pay you back for all of this, as soon as—"

"No. You won't," he said, leaning forward and quickly brushing my cheek with his lips.

By the time we pulled into the little town of Yachats, the sun was setting. It was a picture-perfect seaside village with restaurants and tourist shops dotting the main street.

Tabon took the road that ran along the shoreline and pulled over.

"Did you see that?" he asked.

I shook my head. "I don't think so."

"Just wait, you will." He kept driving another couple of blocks before pulling up to a house with a set of gates similar to those at the duplex in Cambria.

"*This* is your house?" I asked when they opened and he drove through.

"Yep. All mine."

He pulled the car into one of the bays of the four-car garage, turned off the engine, and looked over at me.

"It belonged to my grandparents, but it became mine when my gram passed away a couple of years ago."

"I'm so sorry."

"I still miss her. More when I'm here. Gramps too, but he died when I was still in high school. Ready to go inside?"

I nodded.

"I'll bring your stuff in later. I want you to see the view while there's still some light."

I waited while he unlocked the door and then punched in an alarm code.

"Come in," he said, motioning for me to go ahead of him.

I walked over to the wall of windows in the front of the house and looked out at the Pacific Ocean.

"What do you look at?" I asked, nodding my head at the telescope I saw to the right.

"Whales, mainly. There are always pods of dolphins, seals, and otters out there too."

"Whales?"

"Yep," he answered. "Did you see that?" he asked, pointing.

I shook my head.

"Look again," he said, coming up behind me. "See that bushy stream of misty air? It's called a blow. It's what a whale does when it comes to the surface. Keep your eyes focused on that location, and soon you'll see it again."

I watched and within a couple of minutes, saw what he described.

"Look," he said again. "Did you see them surface?"

"I did. How many are out there?"

"Not sure exactly. There's a family of gray whales that lives here year-round. You'll also see more of them migrating. I've heard something like eighteen thousand travel along this coast twice a year. Once in a while we even see Orcas."

I was mesmerized by the sound of the waves crashing on the rocky shoreline, and captivated by the whales whose blow I saw every few minutes.

"Can I get you anything?"

"No, thank you," I murmured, holding up the binoculars he handed to me.

"How about some water?" he asked.

I thanked him and took a sip from the glass he set on a ledge by the windows.

"It doesn't get too warm here, even in the summer," he said, handing me one of his sweatshirts, even though I had a couple of my own in the car. "The sun will be setting soon, and then it'll get really chilly."

I pulled the sweatshirt over my head and loved that it smelled like him. I looked up; he was studying me. "What?" I asked.

"I've never brought anyone else here."

"No?"

"Never even considered it."

"Why not?"

"Because this place is special to me. Almost sacred, if that makes any sense."

I nodded.

"No one else meant enough to me to share it with. Come here." He pulled me to sit on his oversized sofa. Once I was comfortable, Tabon reached over the cushions and pulled a blanket out of a basket.

"I thought you hadn't spent much time on the East Coast," I said when he covered me with the Hudson Bay wool.

"There's this new thing, I don't know if you've ever seen one…what are they called? Oh yeah, catalogs."

I swatted him and smiled.

"Close your eyes, sweet Avarie. I can't tell you how many nights I've fallen asleep to the sound of waves crashing against the shore. Even when Doc was gone and we didn't know whether he was dead or alive, the sound of the ocean put me to sleep."

Half awake and half asleep, I tried to roll over, but something was keeping me from moving. I opened my eyes to find Tabon's arm and leg wrapped around me from where he slept behind me on the sofa.

Soft light was streaming in through the window blinds, and while the room felt slightly chilly, Tabon did not. When I tried to ease out of his grasp, he groaned and held on tighter.

"No," he murmured. "It is not time to wake up yet, and it is especially not time for you to move."

"But…I need to use the little girls' room."

Tabon moved his leg first and then his arm. "That's the only excuse for getting up this early that I'll accept."

After using the bathroom, I called Aine. It was early, but she wouldn't mind. When my twin didn't answer, I returned to the main room, found the sofa empty, but heard Tabon puttering around in the kitchen. Seconds later came the familiar sound of the one-cup coffee-maker hissing out its steamy brew. I breathed in the heavenly aroma.

I sat at the bar that separated the kitchen and dining room.

"Turn around," he said, setting a cup in front of me and pointing to the windows. "The whales are far more active this time of day. You may even see one breach."

Tabon sat on the stool beside me and stretched his arms over his head until his shirt rode up enough that I could see his rock-hard abs.

"You're supposed to be watching for whales," he said.

"I thought maybe I was supposed to be watching you breach."

He laughed.

I looked out at the water. "There's one." I pointed to a blow.

"Yep. You're getting better at spotting them."

Tabon stood, went back into the kitchen, and opened the refrigerator door.

"How do eggs sound this morning? Maybe some bacon and toast to go along with a serving of sunny-side up?"

I wasn't very hungry, even the talk of food made me queasy. "Whatever sounds good to you is fine with me."

He closed the refrigerator, came back around the bar, and sat next to me.

"What?"

"You aren't hungry."

"I'm sure I will be soon…"

"No, you won't."

I tried to gauge whether he was annoyed with me or simply stating a fact, and how did he know that this time I really wasn't?

"How about a walk on the beach instead?" he asked.

"That sounds really nice."

"Meet you back here in five." He smiled like I imagined he did when he was a little boy.

"Make it ten and you have yourself a walk-on-the-beach partner."

25

Razor

Other than pointing out several oceanfront landmarks, I was quiet for the majority of our walk south. When we reached the mouth of the Yachats River, where it spilled into the ocean, I turned inland.

"There's a great coffee place right over here," I said, motioning toward the hillside.

"Where?" Ava asked.

"You'll see." I took her hand and led her down the dirt pathway.

"You're crazy."

"Be patient, princess."

Ava stopped walking. "Don't call me that, Tabon."

I turned around and looked at her. "Sore spot?"

She nodded. "Very."

"Who called you that, baby?"

She studied me, her eyes didn't blink.

"You can trust me," I murmured.

She crossed her arms and looked back out at the ocean. "My mother."

"Tell me about it." Again, I kept my voice soft, hoping she would share why it affected her in the way it did.

"She didn't use it in a positive way."

I put my arm around her shoulders. "Go on."

"I didn't have an ideal childhood," she said, moving away from me.

"I'm sorry to hear that." I stood my ground next to her, wishing she was still within reach.

"Don't feel sorry for me," she muttered. "Boarding school was the best thing that ever happened to both Aine and me."

When I continued down the dirt trail, Ava followed.

"Tell me about boarding school."

She talked about meeting Tara and Penelope first. "Quinn didn't arrive until a month later."

"Did you know right away that you'd be friends?"

"Definitely." Ava smiled and then talked about their first year together. There was a certain amount of sadness underlying her story, but I sensed it wasn't due to being away from her parents.

"Oh!" she said, suddenly seeing where I'd led her. "It's built into the hillside."

The coffee bar had once been an ice cream place that was, as she'd said, built into the hillside near the estuary. Back in the day, it was a tourist destination, but once the ice cream part of it closed and the coffee business took it over, it became a locals' only hangout.

"Well, if it isn't Razor Sharp," said Andie, the owner.

"Hey, darlin'," I said when she came around from behind the bar to hug me. I caught Ava raise an eyebrow when Andie hung on a little longer than necessary, and winked.

"What can I get you?" she asked, looking only at me.

"Before we order, Andie, I'd like you to meet Ava. Ava, Andie and I went to high school together."

"He was my prom date. We were king and queen, as a matter of fact."

I inwardly cringed and wanted to throttle Andie when I saw Ava's reaction. Was any of that necessary information?

"How's Steve?" I asked.

"You'd have to ask his new girlfriend," she responded, ruining my attempt to let Ava know my one-time prom date was off the market, not that I had any interest in her.

"I'm sorry to hear you aren't still together."

"Sometimes it's meant to be, sometimes it's not, if you know what I mean." When Andie looked directly at Ava, I found myself wishing I'd never brought her to get coffee, at least not here.

"You from around here?"

Ava shook her head. "I'm from New York."

I put my arm around Ava's shoulders. "So, let's order. We have a lot planned this afternoon. What would you like, baby?"

She smirked. "A latte, please, *dah-ling*."

"Oh, are you two…"

I turned my head so I could see Ava's face, surprised by the smile I found there. I'd seen that twinkle in her eye one time before, and knew she was about to let a zinger loose on Andie.

"We haven't told my family yet, so, shh," I said.

"Oh! Right. So a latte for the *young* lady, and Razor, the usual?"

"I'll have a latte too, please."

Andie went back behind the bar, which was exactly what I'd been hoping for.

"I can't wait to hear what Mama Sharp thinks of your new girlfriend. We play mahjong every week with the ladies from book club," Andie said while she worked on our coffee.

"I'm sure she'll love her just as much as I do." I leaned over and kissed Ava's face, right near her temple. "Who wouldn't love her?" I added.

When Andie turned her back, Ava looked at me with scrunched eyebrows.

"It's the truth," I murmured. While most of what I'd said was to fire back at Andie, the last thing wasn't. Ava was very lovable. She wasn't just beautiful. She was smart and funny, the kind of friend who would always be there when she was needed, and even though no one else may see it, I knew exactly how much of the weight of the world Ava carried on her shoulders.

"Ready to head back?" I asked once Andie finished making our coffee drinks.

"It was nice to meet you," Ava said to Andie, giving her a little wave as we walked away.

When they got to the top of the hill, I reached for her latte. "May I?"

"Okay." She handed me her cup.

I set both hers and mine down on the trail and cupped her cheek with my palm. Our eyes met before our lips did. What I saw told me that she was feeling the same heated intensity I was.

The way Ava clung to me made me want to pick her up and carry her back to my house where, after I ravished her body with mine, I'd promised to protect her and keep her safe, not just now, but for the rest of her life.

I remembered the day Mercer and I sat in a bar in the middle of New York City and I realized my friend was in love. He'd been the first of us four to find someone he wanted to spend the rest of his life with. At the time, I doubted the same thing would happen to me. My life wasn't set up to accommodate a relationship, or so I'd thought.

After watching Mercer and Quinn make it work, followed by Doc and Merrigan, I realized that it was possible; all it took was finding a woman who made me want to. Admittedly, I'd thought about Ava in that moment of clarity, but brushed the memory of our brief encounter away.

When I'd left that night—so Mercer could take over Quinn's detail, but also because she still believed I was her boss, not her fill-in bodyguard—I'd stuck around long enough to see if any of Quinn's friends showed up. And they had. I'd caught a glimpse of Ava that night and regretted that I couldn't go back inside, buy her another drink, and spend the evening getting to know the woman I couldn't forget.

A year later, here she was, by my side, her hand in mine. Nowhere in my wildest dreams could I have predicted this outcome.

Once her ex went to trial, and K19 brought down her father, what would be left between us? Would she still want to be with me, or would she celebrate being able to return to the life she led before she became a witness in a trial so much bigger than she could ever imagine?

She'd said she hadn't had an ideal childhood, but I'd seen her with her father, and she loved him. So did her twin. If I was part of the team that not only brought him down, but also exposed his real identity, would either woman ever forgive me?

"I want you to meet my family," I blurted.

"You sure about that?"

"Absolutely. I'll call when we get back to the house and let them know we're in town."

Ava nodded, but seemed distracted. I put my arm around her shoulders. "Tell me what you're thinking."

"It's just…how will you introduce me?"

"Let's see. My girlfriend, my lover, the best thing that ever happened to me. Any of those work for you?"

She smiled and rolled her eyes.

"I could also introduce you as the love of my life."

She wasn't smiling anymore.

"Ava?"

"Don't make fun of me, Tabon."

I stopped walking and turned her body so I could look in her eyes. "How is that making fun of you?"

She tried to shrug away, but I wouldn't let her.

"I get that you don't take…*relationships* seriously. But that doesn't mean you have to make a mockery of them."

"Hey," I said, stroking my finger down the side of her face. "That was awfully presumptive of you, wasn't it?"

"Am I wrong?"

"Couldn't be more so."

"I'm hardly the love of your life, Tabon. You don't even know me."

"I disagree. I know you very well."

"You know *about* me. That's different than knowing me."

"Again, I disagree. I know when you say you're not hungry, you are. And I even know when you really aren't. I know that you make sure the world sees you as independent and completely self-sufficient, and you are anything but. You rely on your sister to reassure you that you are so much more amazing than you know."

"That isn't—"

I stepped closer and could feel her staggered breathing on my face and chest.

"I know how to make your body sing, Ava, in a way that no one else has or will again."

"You have a high opinion of yourself, Tabon."

"You're wrong. The reason no one will again is because I have no intention of ever letting you go."

"You don't mean that."

"Oh, I do, Avarie. Do you think the things I've told you aren't true? I haven't misled you. I've shared things with you that I never thought I'd share with anyone. And I've broken every cardinal rule of my job to take care of you and protect you in a way that I know is risky."

Ava tried again to shrug away from me, and this time, I let her.

"Do you think I'm lying to you, Ava?"

"No. I know you're not."

"How do you feel about me?"

It may not be fair for me to ask when she was in such a vulnerable state, but I had to know. If she didn't think she could love me, I'd be devastated.

"Ava?"

"Don't do this, Tabon."

"What am I doing?"

"You're…this…isn't real."

"It is to me."

26

Razor

I heard sounds of Ava moving about my bedroom, wishing I could wind back the clock and take back everything I'd said to her this morning.

Clearly, she hadn't taken my saying she was the love of my life seriously, but then what twenty-something woman would have when it came from a thirty-something man?

If someone had asked me my thoughts on age a week ago, I would've said it didn't matter. My philosophy had always been, "you're only as old as you feel."

There weren't many days I felt much different than I had at twenty-five, although I did recognize I was more mature. In the last hour, I felt like I'd aged ten years, at least.

How foolish had I been to think someone like Ava—young, beautiful, smart, and funny, just starting out in life—would be as interested in me as I was in her?

She'd actually gone so far as to ask me to stop embarrassing myself. *Don't do this, Tabon,* were her exact words.

I felt like such an idiot that I came downstairs to hide out in my office, telling her I had calls to make. So far, I hadn't made a single one. I needed to get my head back in this mission, because that's what it was. At the end of the day, my assignment wasn't solely to protect Avarie McNamara, it was to bring down the man who'd lied about his identity her whole life.

Shit. Was that what Ava meant when she'd said that I reminded her of her father? *Jesus.* The man was married to a woman younger than she was. She must have been trying to tell me not to make a fool of myself over her, like her father did with his constant stream of younger women.

"Hey," said Gunner, answering my call.

"Where are you?"

"Two doors down on the right."

"Do you think Monk really needs to stick around?"

"Nope. I'm sending him to Seattle."

"Bring me up to speed on the Petrov investigation."

Fifteen minutes later, I was itching to get out of Yachats and back out into the field. I'd never been the lead on asset protection, because everyone knew what I'd refused to acknowledge. If I hadn't been interested in sleeping with Ava, I never would've accepted the assignment in the first place.

"When is Monk leaving?"

"As soon as I can make the arrangements. An hour tops."

"What do you think of him?"

"In what way, Raze?"

"Asset protection."

"I see."

"You want me to tell you that you were right and I was wrong?"

I waited, but Gunner didn't even crack a joke.

"I can't do it, man," I finally said.

"Where is she now?" Gunner asked.

"Upstairs. I'm in my office."

"How do you want to handle the exchange?"

"I have no idea."

"We'll be over in a few minutes, and I'll handle it."

I'd never felt like a bigger pussy than I did right now. I was like a damn dog scurrying away with my tail between my legs. That's not who I was. Was I really going to let a twenty-two-year-old woman bring me to my knees? Hell, no.

I bounded up the stairs to let Miss Avarie know that I'd be much more effective out in the field rather than playing her goddamn nursemaid. I stopped in my tracks when I found the most beautiful woman I'd ever known, sound asleep on my bed.

Sun streamed through the window, casting its rays on her body. If I caressed her skin, I knew it would feel heated, and oh, how I wished I could touch her.

I couldn't be that guy, though, who wanted her more than she wanted me. How many women had I felt the opposite about over the years? The more they tried to convince me how right they were for me, the more I hated being in their presence. Knowing she thought of me that same way made me nauseous.

"Tabon?" she said, rolling over and finding me staring at her.

"I'm sorry I woke you, Ava," I said from the doorway. "There's been a change in plans. Monk will be taking over for me. He'll be here in a few minutes."

She sat up straight and wrapped her arms around her stomach. "Oh. For how long?"

"Indefinitely."

The last thing I expected was for her eyes to fill with tears or for her to try to hide her face from me. As much as she'd hurt my pride when she rejected me, I wasn't that much of an asshole that I'd let her cry and not comfort her.

I strode over to the bed and sat on the edge. "Come here," I said, taking her into my arms.

"I'm sorry…" She gulped. "I'm sure there are more important things than babysitting me."

"It isn't that, Ava. I crossed a line I shouldn't have, and I regret it."

"Oh," she said, pulling away from me and wiping at her tears. "Um, excuse me."

She walked into the bathroom and closed the door behind her. How else should I have said it? *I'm sorry I thought that sex between us meant something. I'm sorry I came on too strong, professing my undying love for you, when we've known each other less than a week. I'm sorry I'm the asshole who thought sex meant love when I'm the one who has been insisting it doesn't all my life.*

When she came out, she had what looked like a toiletry bag in her hand. She walked over to the suitcase she'd left on my bedroom floor, put the bag inside, and zipped it up.

"I'm ready," she said, standing it on end and wheeling it to the doorway.

"Where is everything we bought yesterday?"

She looked at me like she didn't understand the question.

"Didn't you put anything away?"

"Oh," she said again, laying the suitcase flat on the floor and opening the zipper. "I'm sorry."

I knelt down beside her. "Ava, what are you doing?"

"I'm taking the clothes out that you bought. I never should've put them in my suitcase in the first place. I just didn't realize…" She put her head in her hands.

"Stop this." I moved her hands away from her face. I stood, pulling her up with me. "I thought you would've unpacked. That's all. The clothes we bought are yours."

"I can't keep them. I don't want them."

I was about to ask why when I heard the front door open.

"Go away," I shouted.

"Raze?" said Gunner. "Where are you?"

He and Monk came around the corner. Gunner looked down at the suitcase lying open in the doorway of the bedroom and then looked between Ava and me.

"I thought she was staying here."

"She is," I answered. "We need a minute." Both men backed away. "Better yet, you can leave, and I'll call you in a few."

"Roger that." Gunner waved behind him and motioned for Monk to follow.

Ava was back down on her knees, rummaging through the suitcase, pulling out everything that I'd bought the day before, folding it, and putting it in a pile.

"Most of it still has the tags on."

"Leave it, Ava." I took her arm and helped her to her feet a second time. "Come with me."

I led her out to the main room of the house and sat on the sofa, pulling her down next to me.

"Let's talk about this."

She nodded, but looked out the windows instead of at me.

"Please, Ava," I said, and her eyes met mine. "I crossed a line that I shouldn't have, and I—"

"*Don't.* I don't need to hear that you regret having sex with me. I heard you the first time." Her cheeks flushed a bright red, and she looked back out the window.

"That isn't what I meant."

"Whatever you regret about me, Razor, is something I don't need to hear. I hate that I'm so dependent on you. I hate having to be dependent on anyone. I feel horrible about this whole situation and what a burden I am, but…but…*shit.*" She wiped at her tears. "I don't want to fucking cry. This is already the most humiliating day of my life."

She stood and walked over to the window. "Can you call Gunner or whoever, and just ask them to come and get me?"

I walked over and stood next to her. "I didn't mean I regretted having sex with you, Ava. Not at all. I know everything I said this morning made you feel uncomfortable. That's what I regret."

My phone buzzed, but I ignored it. Seconds later, someone pounded on the front door right before Gunner came bursting in, followed again by Monk.

"*What the fuck—*"

"There's a situation," said Gunner.

I put my hand on my gun, waiting for him to continue.

"Not here," he said and motioned to Monk. "Ava, I need to talk to Razor."

She nodded and looked over at Monk warily. I hated leaving in the middle of our conversation, but Gunner wouldn't have burst in the way he had if something wasn't urgent.

"I'll be right back," I said to her before following Gunner downstairs.

"Just heard from Doc. We've lost contact with the sister and their two friends."

"What?"

"You heard me. There's more, Petrov has ghosted as well."

"Who's on the three women?"

Gunner rattled off a couple of names I didn't recognize. "Agency?"

"Not exactly."

"Contractors?"

Gunner nodded.

"Where the hell is Striker?"

"On his way to Seattle."

I ran my hand through my hair, knowing that Gunner was telling me everything he knew, but wanting to pull more information out of him by the throat.

"Trackers?"

"As I said, we've lost contact."

"*What the fuck?*" I paced from one side of my office to the other.

Gunner stood in front of me, looking like the man I'd known more than half my life, but he sure as hell didn't sound like him.

"Wait a minute. Seattle? I thought they were in San Francisco. Gunner, what aren't you telling me?"

This conversation and the one I'd just had with Ava—if anyone could call it a conversation—were so far out of left field, I wondered if this was just a long, strange-ass dream.

"I should've acted sooner."

"What does that mean?"

"I received intelligence I didn't believe was credible."

"Goddammit. Quit making me ask questions."

"There's chatter about Petrov. We aren't the only ones who want to bring him down."

"Who else?"

"The Armenians."

That made sense. Petrov was Azerbaijani, and there was no greater enemy to his people. Tensions had escalated in the early part of this century when it was reported that a prominent Azerbaijan politician met with a municipal delegation from Bavaria, Germany, and stated that their goal was complete elimination of Armenians in the same way the Nazis had tried to eliminate the Jews. Naturally, the German delegation had called for the immediate removal of the politician from their meeting; however, the message communicated couldn't have been more clear.

"You think the Armenians may have taken the three women?"

Gunner nodded. "The source, it appears, is more credible than I initially believed."

"Who's the source?"

"Raketa Ivashov."

"I understand why you questioned her report. What is her involvement?"

"What is her *stated* involvement?"

I nodded.

"She owed us one."

Gunner had saved the life of one of United Russia's most lethal agents a few months back, on one of K19's most complicated missions—the same one during which Gunner had been forced to take down his asset when she'd threatened to kill Doc.

"Does she know their intent?"

"She believes they meant to snatch Ava, but got the wrong twin."

Fuck. "Does she know where the Armenians are taking them?"

"She says she does. That's why Striker is headed to Seattle."

"Where is she now, Gunner?"

"Also on her way to Washington."

"Working with?"

"She's a free agent; she wants to work with us."

I took a seat, processing through everything Gunner had just told me.

Russian agents, particularly those working directly for United Russia, didn't become "free agents." They defected. I could count the ones who had successfully ended their relationship with UR on one hand, and those were dropping like flies, regardless of which country gave them asylum.

Inviting Ivashov to team up on this mission meant that the K19 team would end up on the wrong side of United Russia, and so would the CIA, not that they gave a shit.

"We can't make this decision on our own."

Gunner nodded.

"How much does Doc know about Ivashov's involvement?"

"Nothing."

"Before we call him, tell me this, does Raketa have intel on the guys Striker assigned?"

"Sure does."

"And Petrov? Does she know where he's holed up?"

"Negative on Petrov."

"Any update?" I asked when Doc answered my call.

"Nothing concrete."

"Gunner received intel we want to discuss with you. I'm going to put the call on speaker."

"Roger that. I'll bring Merrigan in as well."

"What's happening?" she asked.

"As I told Doc, Gunner has received intel that he wasn't certain was credible."

Gunner proceeded to reiterate most of what he'd told me.

"I have to admit, I'd heard chatter that Ivashov wanted out. Not an easy feat, given who she works for," said Merrigan.

"Not many live to tell the tale," I added.

"Why does she want out?" Doc asked.

"I can't answer that," said Gunner. "All I know is that she said she owed us one and wants to meet."

"It means opening ourselves up to a shit-ton of trouble."

"I know, Doc."

"But? Come on, Gunner. Give me something to work with here."

"Raketa believes an Armenian faction abducted Aine and the two girls, but not intentionally. The intel indicates they meant to grab Ava."

"What else?"

"They're being transported to Seattle."

"And then where?"

It wouldn't take a genius to figure out the Armenians intended to transport the girls over the border into Canada. Given they had the "wrong twin," K19 might have time to prevent them from leaving the country.

"Do you trust her?" asked Doc.

I understood the reason for Doc's question. It was something we all had to consider. Was Ivashov setting a trap for K19? Was UR in on the search for Petrov?

"Let's talk about Petrov for a minute. When's the last time he was spotted?" asked Merrigan.

"The wedding," answered Gunner. "He got on a plane, allegedly, and no one's seen or heard anything from him since."

"With both his daughters avoiding contact with him, there'd be no one to report anything different," said Doc."Except he never got off the flight. I doubt he was on it in the first place."

That meant he could still be in California. The idea made my skin crawl. At least both of his daughters were no longer there. However, he could very well have been on their tails. The only thing Petrov couldn't know, was where either had traveled once they boarded K19's aircraft.

"Let's get back to Ivashov," said Doc.

"At the minimum, Gunner needs to meet with her. In the meantime, I'll follow up with MI6 to see if they've received further intel on her possible *defection.*"

"Thanks, Fatale," I said.

"What's next, Gunner?"

"The plane is at Wakonda now. The only question is who goes?"

"Razor?" asked Doc.

I'd never been so torn about an assignment. I wanted to get on that plane with Gunner just as much as I wanted to stay here with Ava. If Ivashov's intel was correct, the Armenians had already realized they had the wrong twin, and would soon be on the hunt for the right one.

It wasn't just the Armenians I was worried about. Between her and her former boyfriend, Ava could bring her father's entire organization down, even though she had no idea that's what she'd be doing.

My original assignment had been to keep her safe until she could testify. Sure, it had become much more than that, but that wasn't part of this conversation.

Even if we were able to find Petrov and neutralize him, which in my mind meant assassination, Ava's safety wouldn't be guaranteed until we took his entire organization *and* the Armenians down.

"Send Monk, and whoever else we can mobilize."

"Onyx and Alegria are already here with the plane. Add me and Monk," said Gunner. "Who else?"

"I just received word that Striker and Dutch are both on their way," answered Doc.

Dutch Miller was one of the best operatives employed by the agency. If I had a short list of who I wanted to join K19's team, Dutch would be at the top. Knowing he was with Striker made my decision even easier.

"I'll work on getting backup for you, Raze," Doc added. "I think it would be best for Gunner to head out and leave Monk behind for the time being."

"Roger that."

The only question that remained to be answered in the short term was what and how much I should tell Ava. I didn't need to ask the other three people in the conversation their opinions. I knew they'd say she didn't need to know any of it.

There was one thing I knew that they didn't, however. Ava had the means to contact Aine. If she did, which I expected she had already tried, how long would it be before she panicked about her sister not answering?

"Is that it for now, gentlemen?" asked Doc.

Both Gunner and I answered in the affirmative and disconnected the call.

"Can I ask you something?" I said to Gunner.

"How much to tell her?" he asked.

"There's more, though."

Gunner raised an eyebrow.

"How much did you tell Barbie?"

"That I shouldn't have?"

I nodded.

"Enough that I feel responsible for her death."

27

Ava

I was standing in front of the window, watching the whales, when Tabon and Gunner came back upstairs. I hadn't said a word to Monk, and vice versa. Now, I understood where he'd gotten the name. If what Gunner had alluded to was true, and I would be staying here, I hoped Monk wasn't the one staying with me. But who else was there? Tabon had already told me that the man would be replacing him indefinitely.

"Be in touch," Gunner said to Tabon as he walked out the front door.

I turned around and studied him as he strode toward me. Was this it? Would we say goodbye and never see each other again? God, the idea hurt more than I ever would've dreamed possible. I bit my tongue as hard as I could, trying to keep myself from crying in front of him again.

"Have a seat," Tabon said with a look on his face I'd never seen before.

"I'd rather stand."

"Sit, Ava," he barked and then turned to Monk. "Clear out, but don't go far."

"Yes, sir," were the first two words I'd heard the man say. Having to stay here with him was going to be hell, but at least I could call my sister.

"The situation Gunner alluded to when he stormed in here is serious, Ava. Very serious."

"What happened?"

Tabon took a deep breath, and I saw the same conflict etched on his face that I'd seen every other time I'd asked a question he didn't want to answer.

"When I came to the airport and asked you not to leave, I told you that the case against Dash Finnegan is more complex than anyone had led you to believe."

"I remember," I whispered, wishing I could stop him from saying another word. Whatever he was about to tell me, I sensed was something I didn't want to know.

"There are people who would like to stop you from testifying, which is why K19, me specifically, was given the assignment to protect you."

I nodded.

"There is someone very close to your family, who Dash works for."

I had no idea who Tabon could possibly be talking about. He must not realize that there wasn't *anyone* close to my family. It had always been that way. Aine and I had never met anyone who worked for our father, and our parents hadn't ever socialized. Whether our father did after their divorce, I would have no way of knowing.

"The K19 team has identified the individual, and are currently searching for him in order to turn him in to the appropriate authorities."

I folded my hands in my lap, digging my fingernails into my flesh. *Here it comes.*

"We aren't the only people looking for him. There is another…team…who wants to find him before we do, and maybe even more than we do. That same group would be very interested in knowing what you know. Do you understand what I mean?"

I closed my eyes and nodded again. "What are you trying to tell me? Please, just say it."

"We believe that group has abducted Aine and, with her, Penelope and Tara."

The sound that came roaring from my chest didn't sound human. I felt Tabon's arms around me, rocking me gently while what my brain could only identify as shrieks of anguish tore their way out of my body.

"I tried to call. She didn't answer," I sobbed.

This was *my* fault. If I hadn't gone looking for Dash that night, none of this would be happening.

"Oh my God—they wanted me, didn't they? They didn't want Aine."

"There is intel to suggest that is true."

"Give me to them, and make them let Aine go. Pen and Tara too. Just give me to them," I cried.

"Shh," Tabon repeated.

Finally, I pulled away from him. "You don't understand, Tabon. I can't live without Aine."

"And she can't live without you."

"I don't fucking care. Aren't you listening to me? Give me to them."

"That won't save your sister or your friends. All that will accomplish is they'll have all four of you. That's it, Ava. Martyring yourself will do *nothing*."

I forced myself to take several deep breaths. Once Tabon left, I'd figure it out on my own. Maybe I could talk to Dash's lawyer, and he could deliver a message, telling whoever had Aine that I wouldn't testify as long as they let her go.

"When are you leaving?" I asked.

"I'm not."

"Why not? You have to find her."

"I'm needed more here."

"For me? You've got to be kidding. I don't matter. Aine is all that matters. *You* have to find her."

"I'm not leaving, Ava."

<h1 style="text-align:center">28</h1>

Razor

She stalked to the window. "I don't matter," she said again, making me want to tear my heart out of my chest. "If you won't look for her, I'll do what I should've done in the first place."

"What is that?"

"Call my father, and then call the police."

I scrubbed my face with my hand. "I can't let you do that."

"As I said—"

"I'm serious, Ava. You can't."

"Like I'm not serious? Jesus, Razor, somebody has my sister. *My sister!* Do you even have a sister?"

Her eyes filled with tears, and as much as I wanted to put my arms around her and tell her it would be okay, I knew she wouldn't allow me to.

"I do have a sister, and if anything like this ever happened to her, I'd want the best people possible to rescue her, and that is the K19 team. You cannot involve your father or the police."

"Can you hear yourself? You're telling me not to tell my parents or get law enforcement involved? Have you all operated in your own little world so long that you've forgotten how real life works?"

I stepped closer. "You have no idea how many lives are saved by the people who you think operate in their own little world."

She stood with her arms crossed, shooting daggers at me.

"If we hadn't done our job, Quinn never would've married Mercer. And Merrigan? She'd be dead just like Quinn would have been. Unless you want that to be your fate and that of your sister and your friends, you're going to do exactly what I tell you to do."

"And if I don't?"

"You will. One way or another."

"Is that a threat?"

"Nope, it's a promise."

"I hate you," she spat.

"That is crystal clear."

I set Monk up in one of the downstairs guest bedrooms and switched the alarm to the stay setting. For the time being, Ava was essentially a captive in my house.

"What are you doing?" I asked when I saw her move her suitcase to a room farther down the hallway. I was pissed when she didn't respond, but for now, I'd let it go. It hadn't been that long since she told me she hated me.

As far as I knew, she hadn't eaten yet, although the news that her sister and friends were missing had likely killed her appetite.

I went into the kitchen and opened and closed the refrigerator. I didn't have much of an appetite either. What I really needed was a good, hard workout. I'd love it if Ava would go for a run with me, but I knew she'd turn me down if I asked.

Instead, I went into the bedroom, changed into workout clothes, and went downstairs, to the gym. I was surprised to hear someone pounding away on the treadmill, particularly since I'd just passed Monk in the hallway. Evidently, Ava had had the same idea I had.

I went back upstairs and called the only person I knew who could give me advice about my current situation without giving me too much shit about it at the same time.

"Hey, Sis," I said when she answered the phone.

"I heard a rumor you were in town."

"Yeah, about that—"

"No worries, Raze. We also heard you weren't alone."

My sister, Saylor, was my only sibling, and from the time we were kids, she'd rarely let anything bother her. I was that way too, which was why I'd initially been recruited for special ops. We both took after our mom.

Our dad was another story. His temper had been legendary in a town as small as Yachats. Ultimately, his inability to handle stress was what killed him. It was almost ten years ago that he'd died of a heart attack.

"That's why I'm calling. I need some advice."

"I'm here if you want to come by."

"I'm housebound right now. Would you mind coming to me?"

"Oh, goodie! Does this mean I get to meet her, whoever she is?"

"Uh…maybe. She isn't speaking to me at the moment."

"I'll be right there. Oh, can I bring the girls along? They'd love to see you."

Sierra and Savannah were a year apart in age, just like Saylor and me. It was hard to believe it was almost six months since I'd last seen them, and then it had been for a quick three-day weekend trip.

29

Ava

I was halfway into what I'd hoped would be a ten-mile run. Staying focused for the amount of time that would take on a treadmill required a great deal of concentration, which I didn't have today. Even the music playing through my headphones, which was turned up far too loud, wasn't enough to drown out the last words *Razor* and I had said to each other.

Giving up, I stopped at six miles and decided that was good enough for now. I wondered if Monk was a runner, since it was unlikely I'd be allowed out of the house without one of them. Since I never wanted to see Razor's face again, Mr. Mute was my only option.

I shrugged when I didn't see him on my way out of the gym. Maybe I'd find him later. For now, I needed a long, hot shower.

Praying Razor wasn't in the main room or the kitchen, I slowly climbed the stairs, keeping my eyes downcast, just in case.

When I came to the landing between floors, I heard what sounded like peals of laughter. I looked up, and two little girls, both blonde and blue-eyed, were standing at the top of the stairs, staring at me.

"Hi," I said, taking my earbuds out.

"Who are you?" one of the girls asked.

I couldn't speak. It was like I was looking at a living, three-dimensional photo of Aine and me when we were little.

"Are you twins?" I managed to eek out, but the two little girls were already racing back to whatever had them captivated before they saw a stranger coming upstairs.

"Hi," said a woman who looked so much like Razor, she had to be his sister. "I'm Saylor, and those two towheads are my girls, Savannah and Sierra."

"Hi," I said, shaking the woman's outstretched hand. "I'm Ava."

I looked beyond the woman, and saw Razor sitting on the floor, letting the two little girls, who couldn't be more than five, climb all over him.

"Are they twins?" I asked again.

"No. Savannah is just tall for her age. They're actually a year apart, like Razor and I are."

"Oh. You call him Razor?"

The woman laughed. "Pity the person who dares call him Tabon."

"Ava calls me Tabon," he said, walking over and standing next to his sister. "Unless she's mad at me."

It wasn't that I was mad at him; I hated him. Didn't I? God, he'd infuriated me, and yet, here I was, wishing he'd take me in his arms again.

"Hey, girls, it's time for us to go and leave Uncle Razor alone for a bit."

"Please don't leave on my account," I said. "I was just about to take a shower."

"I don't want to go," whined one of the girls. I wasn't sure if she was Savannah or Sierra. "I wanna stay with Uncle Razor and Aunt Ava," she said, coming up and putting her teeny hand in mine.

"I'm so sorry," said Saylor, trying to get the little girl to let go. "Come on, Sierra. Remember that I promised to take you to see Ya-Ya after we saw Uncle Razor?"

"I don't want to go see Ya-Ya," said the other girl. "I want to stay here." She proceeded to join her sister, holding my other hand with both of hers.

"Who's Ya-Ya?" I asked, kneeling down so I was on their level.

"She's their grandmother. Our mom," Saylor said, looking back at Razor. "She wasn't quite ready to be called Grandma."

"My mother would never be ready to be called Grandma either. She doesn't even let us call her Mom."

Saylor laughed. "What's her replacement name?"

"Peggy," I deadpanned.

"Who wants to play frisbee on the beach?" asked Razor.

Both little girls cheered, but neither let go of my hands.

"I'm sorry," he mouthed.

I could barely look at him. Not only because I was mad, but because he'd changed into workout clothes just like the ones he'd worn when we went for our run in Cambria. The same clothes I'd stripped off his sweaty body before he did the same and brought me to orgasm after orgasm.

I closed my eyes, remembering what he'd said earlier.

I know how to make your body sing, Ava, in a way that no one else has or will again. The reason no one will again is because I have no intention of ever letting you go.

Had he meant those words? Did I really matter to him, and would I still after this nightmare ended?

"Come on," I heard him say, taking each girl's hand in his. When they let go, I missed the warmth and comfort they'd given me.

"Wanna come along?" he asked.

I nodded, still unable to find my voice with him.

"I thought they were twins," I told him after we'd been on the beach long enough that the girls had lost interest in playing frisbee and were in the water instead.

"I can understand why you would've thought that. It'll only be a minute before Savannah is taller than Sierra."

"I'm sorry for what I said earlier. I don't hate you."

"I know you don't, and I knew you didn't when you said it. And you were right, if something like what you're going through ever happened to Saylor, the only way anyone could stop me from trying to find her would be to shackle me."

"I'm so scared." I sat on the sand and lowered my head. Tabon sat next to me.

"Come here," he said, putting his arm around me and drawing me close to him.

There wasn't a single thing I could think of that would feel better right now, except a hug from my sister.

"I asked Saylor to come over to get her advice."

"What about?"

"You."

"I was afraid you were going to say that. Has Saylor been a bodyguard too? I know that isn't what you really do, but you know what I mean."

"No, but she's always given me the best advice when it came to girls I liked."

I stared out at the waves. It was low tide, so they rolled in gently, rather than crashing against the rocks on the shoreline. "What was her advice?" I asked without looking at him.

"To give you space, but never be too far away. Be smart enough to know when you need me to leave you alone and when, instead, to give you a hug."

"Does she know about…you know?"

"No. And she wouldn't ask."

"So, she thinks I'm a bitch?"

"Saylor is the least judgmental person I know."

"Aine is like that."

Tabon nodded. "I want you to understand I know how hard this is for you. I truly believe our team will find your sister and bring her back safe, or I would've been on that plane myself."

"But you stayed with me instead."

"I did." Tabon scrubbed his face with his hand. "Do you not understand that I couldn't live with myself if anything happened to you?"

"I'm sorry," I whispered, again trying so hard not to cry.

"There's nothing for you to be sorry for. I get that you think I'm this annoying guy who has the hots for you, but it's so much more than that for me, Ava. There hasn't been a day since I met you that you haven't popped into my head at least once."

"I don't think that about you."

He laughed. "Right."

"Tabon." I waited until he was looking at me. "I don't think that about you," I said a second time.

Again, he turned away from me, only this time, I could see the hurt in his eyes.

"You asked me to stop," he said.

"When?"

"I was telling you how I feel about you, and you said it wasn't real."

"That's not what I meant."

"No? I didn't mishear you, Ava."

I drew my knees up close to my body and wrapped my arms around them.

"You were a fantasy, Tabon. My fantasy. There wasn't a breath you took the day I met you that I don't remember. I've played every word you said to me over and over in my head."

"Fantasies rarely live up to the hype."

"Are you fishing for a compliment?"

"Hardly. I'm being realistic, Ava."

"Don't call me that."

He turned his head and looked at me and I smiled. "No one ever calls me Avarie, except you."

"I hate it when you call me Razor."

"I know, and you're right. I only call you that when I'm mad at you. I do it in my head too."

"What do you mean?"

"I always think of you as Tabon, but when I'm mad, you're Razor in my head."

"I guess that's better than 'asshole.'" He leaned closer. "Can I kiss you, Avarie?"

I nodded, and he covered my lips with the sweetest, most gentle kiss. How could I have told this man that I hated him? Especially since all he'd ever wanted to do was protect me?

"Okay, you two," said Saylor. "The girls are tired, so I'm going to take them home, but—"

"What?" Tabon asked.

I looked up at his house like his sister was.

"Who is *that*?"

"That's Monk. He's hangin' with us for a few days."

"Someone you work with?"

Tabon nodded.

"He's kinda hot."

For the first time since we'd met, I looked at Saylor's left ring finger and saw it was bare.

"I'll explain later," Tabon whispered.

It wasn't any of my business, and I'd certainly seen plenty of people divorce in my life. My father alone had done it three times.

"He doesn't talk very much," I said to Saylor. "I think I've heard him say a total of three words."

"Is that why you call him Monk?"

Tabon nodded.

"I can live with that, as long as he's not celibate too."

30

Razor

"You moved your stuff out of the room," I said when we walked back into the house.

"It's your room, Tabon."

What was I supposed to do now? Should I tell her I wanted her to sleep with me, or should I give her space? She was obviously distraught over her sister and her friends. I didn't want her to think I was coming on to her at a time like this.

"You could invite me back," she murmured.

"Wait. What? Of course I want you with me. I was just trying to figure out if saying so would make me too much of an asshole."

"I don't think I'd be able to sleep…you know…alone."

"You don't have to, baby."

"Look," she said pointing out the window. "There are two side by side."

I didn't see the blow, but I saw the two whales as they momentarily surfaced, and she was right, they were side by side.

"You've got to be starving," I said, walking into the kitchen. "You haven't eaten anything all day."

"I wasn't hungry, but now I think I could eat something little."

"How about eggs and toast?"

"That sounds perfect."

"Bacon?"

Ava scrunched her nose.

"That would be no bacon."

"Hey," said Monk, coming up the stairs. "Am I interrupting?"

"Not at all. I was about to make eggs and toast if you'd like to join us."

Monk walked over and opened the refrigerator, pulling things out and setting them on the counter.

"I could make omelets if you'd like," he offered.

"You cook?"

Monk nodded. "I spent a year undercover as a private chef."

"That would be awesome. Seriously. I can't cook for shit."

I looked over and saw a smile show through Ava's haunted eyes. No matter how brief, I loved seeing it.

"Avarie, you think you could manage an omelet, or would you prefer to stick with plain eggs?"

This time the smile wasn't as brief. "I'd love an omelet. Thanks, Monk."

"Uh, you're welcome, Avar—"

"That's it. Just Ava. I'm the only one who calls her Avarie."

Monk went back to chopping vegetables, but I swore he smiled too.

"Damn, you're a good cook," I said, rubbing my belly.

"Chef."

"Oh, sorry, Monk. Maybe we should start calling you that instead."

"Chef Monk is fine with me."

"So, Monk. Are you single?" Ava asked.

"Excuse me?"

"You know…not married, not dating anyone."

Monk looked at me and then back at Ava. "Yeah. Single."

"Are you gonna tell him anything else, or just leave him hangin'?"

"I wasn't sure I should."

"My sister has the hots for you, Monk. Beware, though. She comes with two of the sweetest little girls on the face of the earth."

Monk nodded, but didn't say anything. A minute later, he stood and went into the kitchen.

I heard the water running. "Hey, you cooked; I'll clean up."

"I got it," he answered. "Your sister. Was she the one here earlier?"

"Yep."

"She's pretty."

I winked at Ava. "My mom's gotta be chomping at the bit to have us over for dinner. We'll get Saylor to bring the girls, and we'll bring Monk along with us."

"Saylor? That's her name?"

I nodded.

"Cool name," said Monk before he turned back to the dishes.

Ava joined him at the sink. "I can help."

"I prefer if you didn't. I like doing dishes. It relaxes me."

"Hey, Tabon? You should invite your sister back over now. A man who cooks the way Monk does who also likes doing dishes? She should grab him before someone else does."

I watched her expression change from playful back to somber. I knew the transition well. When Gunner, Mercer, and I all believed that Doc had been killed in action, every smile was followed by a somber moment of regret. It was a horrible way to live for those two years, until we discovered he'd been held captive by a group of Russians. Finding out he was still alive was one of the best days of my life.

Soon, I prayed, Ava could smile with the same sense of relief, knowing her sister was safe.

"Would it be okay if I took a shower?" Ava asked.

"Of course."

"I was on my way, earlier, after my run, when I met your sister and nieces."

"It's okay. You don't have to ask, Avarie."

"Thanks."

I watched her walk to my bedroom door, where she turned back around.

"Coming?" she asked.

"You know it. I'll be right there."

Ava nodded and closed the door behind her.

"Any news?" I asked Monk.

"The last update I received, Gunner hadn't made contact with Ivashov yet."

"Keep me posted."

I hadn't thought to ask Gunner where Raketa was traveling from when he said she was on her way to Seattle. It could be hours before they connected if she was coming from Russia. Although, that wouldn't make sense. No agent in their right mind would risk divulging what she'd told Gunner if she were still in her country.

Gunner had a shit-ton of backup, not that he couldn't handle Raketa on his own, but if she was setting a trap, at least he wasn't alone.

I slipped inside the bedroom door, and could see Ava in the bathroom, undressing. I would've preferred peeling those clothes off her gorgeous body myself, but watching was pretty nice too.

She seemed lost in thought. Was she thinking about Aine? As much as I hoped she wasn't, how could she not be? There was a very real possibility that her sister had been abducted in her place. How could she not feel the burden that knowledge brought with it?

I took off my clothes where I stood, and walked into the bathroom.

"Oh," she gasped. "I didn't hear you come in."

When she looked me up and down, I couldn't tell if she was admiring what she saw or wondering what the hell I was doing.

She opened the glass door of the shower, but didn't close it behind her, so I followed her in.

"Tabon," she said, wrapping her arms around my neck. "Have I told you how much I love that name?"

"I always hated it until I heard it from your sweet lips."

I picked up the body wash and drizzled some on my hands, rubbing them together to make a lather. I started with her neck, massaging her tense muscles with my soapy hands. Ava closed her eyes and leaned back against the tile.

"That feels so good."

I made my way down the front of her body, taking one of her heavy breasts in my hands and giving it all of my attention. When the first was rosy pink from the warm water, I moved to the other, lavishing it the same way.

Slowly, I moved over her stomach, and then knelt in front of her. I drizzled more body wash on my hands and rested them near the top of her thighs.

"Open, baby," I breathed.

Slowly and gently, I caressed her folds with my fingertips, until I heard her whimper. "Tabon, please," she begged.

"Tell me what you want, Avarie."

"Your fingers, inside me."

I held her still with one hand on the cheek of her ass while I sunk into her heat with two fingers of the other.

"Is this what you want, baby?"

Her hands landed on my shoulders, and she leaned forward, supporting her weight on me.

"God, yes," she mewled.

"Come for me." I thrust harder into her softness, circling her bud of nerves with my thumb.

I felt her clamp down on my fingers at the same time she dug her nails into the skin of my shoulders. I held her still as her body pulsed against my hand.

She tried to get me to stand, but I wasn't finished.

I slowly moved my fingers back to her folds, gently caressing them again.

"Lean against the wall, Avarie." I poured more body wash into my hands and massaged her legs, one by one, working my fingers into the tight muscles. Tomorrow I needed to make sure she was able to get a long run in before she got any tighter. It would also help her burn off some of the debilitating stress she was under.

"Turn around and rest your forearms against the tile."

She did as she was told, and I continued massaging her legs, up to her delectable bottom. I couldn't resist leaning forward and nibbling her sweet butt cheek. Again, she whimpered, sending all the blood to my groin.

I stood and massaged the muscles of her back until both hands rested on her shoulders.

"Oh my God, Tabon. I can't even…"

"Let's wash your hair. Turn around for me."

When she did, her eyes met mine. "Why are you being so sweet to me?" she whispered. "I was horrible to you today."

I shook my head. "I told you I'd take care of you, Avarie, and I meant it. That doesn't mean only when you're nice to me; it means whenever you need it. Sometimes you need it more when the world isn't giving you any reason to be sweet."

"Tabon…I…I…"

I covered her lips with mine, thrusting my tongue into her mouth and taking the words she wasn't ready to say inside my body. I pulled back and rested my forehead against hers.

"Sweet Avarie," I murmured. "I do too."

After our shower, we sat and watched the sun as it set on the ocean, and counted the number of times we spotted whales. Soon her eyes were drifting closed.

"Come on, baby," I said, taking her hand. "Let's get you into bed."

She stood still as I unzipped her jeans, pulled them off with her panties, and then pulled the sweatshirt over her head. Next, I unfastened her bra. I pulled back the covers, and she crawled between the sheets.

"I like your bed, Tabon."

I smiled. "My bed likes you too. Almost as much as I do." I crawled in and wrapped my arm around her, drawing her close so her head rested on my chest.

"Sleep, baby," I whispered, stroking the skin on her back.

"Tabon?"

"Yes, Avarie?"

"Will Gunner get my sister back? Pen and Tara too?"

"Yes, he will. I promise."

I couldn't toss or turn, or even get up to get a glass of milk. I could, but I wouldn't, not with Ava asleep in my arms.

I'd probably be asleep too if I hadn't made her a promise that Gunner would rescue Aine, Penelope, and Tara. Yes, I believed he would. I had complete faith in him and the rest of the team we'd assembled. I'd just feel a hell of a lot better if I heard something.

When my phone pinged and also vibrated on the bedside table, I grabbed it, trying to silence it before it woke Ava.

Thankfully, when I moved, she did too, rolling over. I'd roll with her, and spoon her from behind, once I checked my messages.

Intel indicates Petrov is on the move.

To?

Unknown.

Fuck. I slipped out of the bed and closed the bedroom door behind me.

"I was hoping you'd respond sometime tonight," said Doc when he answered my call.

"It was less than five minutes, asshole."

"How's Ava?"

"Shaky at best. Thankfully, asleep."

"Merrigan received the intel from MI6. Shiver is also on his way."

Marquess Thornton "Shiver" Whittaker was one of the best operatives, not just in MI6, but in all of the UK. After Dutch, he'd be the second person I would want to partner with K19.

"What have you heard from Seattle?"

"Gunner is meeting with Raketa now."

"Alone?"

"That was her condition."

If this was a trap and anything happened to Gunner, I would personally hunt down Raketa Ivashov and kill her with my bare hands.

"Anything else I should know?"

"I'd get ready to move again."

I'd already begun thinking about it. Without knowing where Petrov was headed, it would be best if we didn't stay in one place very long.

31

Ava

I'd come so close to telling Tabon I loved him earlier. But I was unable to bring myself to say the words. I meant them, though.

If anyone had ever asked if I believed in love at first sight, I would've scoffed. Now, I knew better. I'd loved Tabon Sharp since I first laid eyes on him. I didn't care if no one believed me—except him, when, one day, I finally got the nerve to tell him.

When I rolled over and reached for him, the other side of the bed was empty and cold, which meant he had to have been gone for some time.

I looked around for something to put on and realized I'd left my suitcase in the other room. It only took two tries before I found the dresser drawer where Tabon kept his t-shirts. Grabbing the one on top, I thought about looking for the panties I'd taken off before our shower, but since Tabon's shirt came almost to my knees, I didn't bother.

Padding out to the main room of the house, I didn't see or hear him. Guessing he was downstairs in his office, I pulled one of the kitchen barstools over near the windows and looked out at the moonlight's reflection on the water.

"What are you thinking about?" Tabon asked, coming up behind me and resting his hands on my shoulders.

I leaned back and rested my head against his chest. "My sister. I just feel so…too many things to put into words. I feel guilty, and I'm terrified for her, especially knowing that I was who they were after, but they got her instead. I'm so scared, Tabon."

"I know, sweetheart. I wish I had more to tell you, but at this point, all I know is that Gunner and the rest of the team are doing everything they can to get her and your two friends back safe and sound."

"I just…"

"Tell me." He wrapped his arms around my waist.

"I wish I could talk to her."

"You can, and if you stop and listen, I bet you'll hear her answer."

"Is that what you did with Doc?"

"Every day. He and I served together for years before we retired to start K19. He's like a brother to me."

I loved how Tabon's arms felt around me. There hadn't been another time in my life when I felt as safe as I did with him. Not that I'd ever thought much about my safety.

"Quinn told me this is how Mercer makes her feel."

I felt Tabon nod.

"Let's go back to bed, Avarie." He kissed my neck and down to my shoulder.

"Make me forget, Tabon. Even for just a little while."

"Avarie…"

"Please, Tabon."

He held my hand in his, led me back to his bedroom, and closed the door behind us.

There was enough light in the room that I could see his eyes as he backed me up until my knees touched the edge of the mattress.

He grasped the hem of his shirt, pulled it over my head, and then ran his hands down my nakedness.

Tabon's eyes focused on mine and then on my lips. When I raised my hand to touch him, he grasped it, brought it to his mouth, and kissed the center of my palm. I shuddered when he pressed the tip of his tongue where his lips had been.

He dropped my hand and cupped my cheek, lowering his mouth to mine. When he nipped my bottom lip, I opened to him, and his tongue swept inside.

"Stay where you are," he said when I leaned back. "I'm exploring." He ran his hands over my body, kissing and nibbling as he went.

He groaned and tongued one of my hardened nipples. I arched forward for more.

"Lie back, put your feet on the bed, and drop your knees for me." He knelt down and spread me open wider. "Put your legs over my shoulders, Avarie." He ran his tongue through my wetness and sunk his fingers inside me.

"Tabon," I whimpered, rolling my head from side to side.

"I need to be inside you," he groaned, positioning himself at my entrance. He thrust into me, and I went off like a firecracker.

A few seconds later, he started again, slowly building his pace until he was thrusting so hard my body trembled and I dug my fingernails into his skin.

I broke apart again, spasming around him. With a roar of pleasure, he stilled and shuddered.

Tabon slid out of me and pulled me close. "Avarie?"

"Mmm. God, Tabon. What you do to me."

"Baby, we…I…didn't use a condom."

"I'm on the pill, Tabon."

"I've never…"

"I've never either. Are you okay?" I asked when he started to pull away from me.

"I'm sorry," he said, cuddling me close again. "I'm fine. Way better than fine." He kissed my forehead.

I groaned, remembering how Tabon had woken me up a second time last night and wrung every ounce of pleasure he could from my body.

I looked at the time, shocked that it was after ten. I found the t-shirt I'd worn the night before on the floor, put it on, and padded out, in search of the man who not only rocked my world, but was also quickly taking command of my heart.

"There she is." Tabon looked up from his laptop and smiled. He opened his arms, and I walked into them.

"You are so beautiful." He cupped my cheek with his palm and brought his lips to mine.

"How long have you been up?"

"Only about an hour." He pointed over to a plate covered with foil on the counter. "That's yours. I couldn't wait. Monk made pancakes and bacon. The smell woke me up."

I took the foil off the plate; the food was still warm. "I'm going to need another run after this."

"I was hoping you'd say that. Coffee?" he asked.

"I'd love some."

As hard as I tried not to think about my sister every minute of the day, every time I felt happy, guilt reared its ugly head.

"Everything okay?" he asked, setting the cup in front of me.

"I know we already talked about this, but whenever I start to feel…I can't help feeling guilty about Aine, Pen, and Tara."

"For every smile, there are ten tears," he said. "I get it. Better than most."

I stretched and rubbed my tummy. "I'm soooo full."

"Ready to run?" Tabon put his hands on my waist and lifted me off the barstool. "Let's work off our pancakes so we have room for whatever Monk makes for dinner."

"We can go as soon as I clean up."

"Doing dishes relaxes Monk, remember?"

32

Razor

This time, I didn't stop and suggest we turn around until Ava did, and by then, we'd gone more than seven miles.

While we ran, we talked about Yachats and how much I'd loved growing up in the small coastal town.

"I really like it here, too."

"Most people complain about how cloudy and cold it is."

Ava shrugged. "It doesn't bother me. There are too many other things about it that make it special."

I smiled. "Having you here with me, makes it more special."

When we stopped to stretch, I saw I'd missed a call from Monk.

"What's up? We were just about to head back."

"Someone got to Dash Finnegan last night. He's dead."

"Fuck," I spat under my breath. I looked up, and something caught my eye—an SUV parked in one of the scenic overlooks.

"Shit. We need cover. There's a four-wheeler in the garage."

"Roger that," said Monk. "I've got your coordinates. On my way."

I looked up again and spotted a drone.

"This way," I said, walking inland, toward the cliffs where there was a trail that would lead us through the sea caves. "Monk is on his way to meet us."

"Why?" Ava asked.

"Just keep moving, baby."

We rounded a corner, and Ava gasped when a woman stepped in front of us.

"Jesus." I jumped. "What in the hell are you doing here?" I asked Alegria.

"Doc."

"We're being tracked. I spotted a drone and an SUV."

"We're the drone."

"Where are we going?" I asked when she led us in a direction different than I would've gone.

"Shortcut," she answered.

A few minutes later, we exited the caves at one of the beach's public parking areas. Onyx was waiting in an SUV while Monk sat nearby on the four-wheeler.

I hurried Ava into the vehicle and climbed in beside her while Alegria got in the front passenger seat. Monk was already on his way back up the beach, to the house.

Onyx looked at me in the rearview mirror. "I guess you know we have company."

"How in the hell did they find us?" Before Onyx answered, I figured it out. *"Jesus Christ, the suitcase,"* I muttered. *Fuck.*

I'd told Ava, on our way back from the airport in San Luis Obispo, that I'd do a sweep of her belongings when we returned to the house in Cambria, but I hadn't ever done it. It was an amateur mistake, one that now put her life in more danger than before.

"Where's the plane?" I asked when Onyx went south on the highway. "Florence?"

"Affirmative."

"I need her phone," Alegria said from the front seat.

"It's at the house."

"No, it isn't." Ava pulled the phone I gave her in Cambria out of a pocket in her shorts and put it in the woman's outstretched hand.

"Yours too," she said to me.

I handed mine over and watched as she dismantled both of them.

"Anything?" I asked.

"Negative."

"Good. Anybody behind us?"

"Not yet," Onyx answered.

"Turn left at the next light. In a quarter mile, take Highway 39 on the right. Immediately after, make a left and then another quick right. You'll see a warehouse. Pull behind it."

Onyx went where I told him to, parked for a few minutes, but no other vehicles passed the warehouse.

"Go out here." I pointed to another exit. "When you hit the two-mile marker, pull off on the left side of the road."

When he did, I opened the door. "Come on," I said to Ava.

"Sir?" asked Onyx.

"Proceed according to the original plan. Fly from Florence to Eugene and wait to hear from me."

"Roger that."

"Go," I said, closing the door behind me.

"What's going on?" Ava asked. "There's nothing here."

"Sure there is." I motioned to a trail that went through the woods.

"Will you tell me where we're going?"

"You'll see in a minute."

A few hundred feet later, the woods opened to a clearing where a cabin sat. I walked to the door, reached up to the ledge above it, and pulled down a key.

"This was my dad's fishing cabin," I said, opening the door.

I walked through the musty space, opening windows as I went. When I reached the back, I waved Ava closer. "Look," I said, pointing out to the lake.

"It's beautiful," she murmured.

"Sorry about all the dust. I don't know when anyone was here last."

Ava walked into the kitchen and opened up the refrigerator door. "Does it work?" she asked.

I shrugged. "Plug it in, and we'll see."

She opened up a couple of the downstairs windows while I went upstairs to do the same.

"It really isn't that bad," she commented, which made me laugh. "I'm serious," she added. "Give me twenty minutes, and it'll look a lot better."

"What can I do to help?" I asked, unable to contain my smile.

"Do you know if there's a vacuum hidden somewhere?"

I didn't, but I looked and found it in the downstairs bedroom closet. I picked up the rotary phone that sat on the bedside table, stunned to hear a dial tone.

"Hey, Sis," I said when Saylor answered.

"Hey, Raze. What's up?"

"I need your help with something."

"Sure. What can I do?"

I told her where we were and that I needed her to make contact with Monk. "Tell him I need two phones. He'll understand what to do."

"Roger that," she joked. "Anything else?"

"I'm not sure how long we'll be here. We might need some provisions." I rattled off a list.

"On my way," she said. "Be there as soon as I can."

I went back out to the main room and saw that Ava had made considerable progress getting the place cleaned up.

"My sister is on her way."

Ava cringed.

"What's wrong?"

"I'm just…" She looked down at her clothes. "Dirty."

I walked over and put my arms around her waist. "Just the way I like you, baby."

"Stop." She laughed but didn't move away from me.

"We could take a shower."

"And put my dirty clothes back on? Yuck."

"Good thing I asked Saylor to bring you something to change into. Several somethings, as a matter of fact."

Ava moved my arms from around her waist. "Tabon, what happened back there?"

Once again, I struggled with what I could tell her. "I had reason to believe we were being followed."

She raised an eyebrow and put her hands on her hips. "What?"

"Tell me the truth."

"That is the truth."

"Who was following us?"

"I'm not certain."

"You know what…never mind."

Before I realized what was happening, she went into the bedroom and closed the door.

"Ava?" I said, trying to turn the knob, but it was locked.

"Go away, Razor."

I had no idea what just happened, but that Ava had called me Razor meant whatever it was, was bad. Thank goodness Saylor was already on her way here.

I walked out of the cabin, stunned to see Saylor wasn't alone. She hadn't thought to ask me if it was okay for her to bring our mother and my two nieces with her?

"Where's Ava?" Saylor asked, getting out of her Jeep.

"Uh…she's calling me Razor again."

My sister burst out laughing. "Uh-oh."

"It's so good to see you," my mother said, putting her arms around my waist.

"Where's Aunt Ava?" asked Savannah, climbing out of the back seat.

"She's inside," I answered and then made eye contact with Saylor. "Help," I mouthed.

"What's going on?" our mother asked.

"I told you, Mom. She only calls him Razor when she's pissed at him. Otherwise, he's Tabon."

"Oh dear." She turned and looked wistfully at the cabin. "A lot of happy memories were made in this place."

I agreed. "Some of the best times of my life."

"What did you do to make her mad?"

"I don't know, Mom. No clue."

"Tell me what happened," said Saylor, sitting down on the porch step.

"Come on, girls," said our mom. "Let's go see the lake."

Savannah dug her heels in. "No, Ya-Ya, I want to see Aunt Ava."

"Shh, Aunt Ava is sleeping right now. You don't want to wake her up, do you?" Saylor put her finger in front of her mouth and motioned toward the lake. "You can see her when you come back up."

"Okay," both girls said, taking their grandmother's hands.

"All right, they're gone. Tell me what happened. Word for word."

I reiterated our conversation.

"Stop."

"What?"

"Do you know who was following you?"

"I have a fairly good idea."

"But you told her you didn't know."

"What was I supposed to tell her?"

"The truth."

"I can't, Saylor. There's a good reason why I can't."

"Why didn't you just say that?"

"Because I was afraid she'd keep asking questions."

Saylor raised her eyebrow and went inside, leaving me no less confused than when she got there.

33

Ava

I couldn't believe *Razor* had lied to me *again.* When we were in the SUV and Onyx asked if he knew they had company, his immediate response had been, "How in hell did *they* find us?"

Yet he'd just told me he wasn't certain who was following us. Making it worse, I'd only seen that expression before when I knew he was lying.

I'd accept it if he said there were things he couldn't tell me, but he'd lied outright, and that, I wouldn't.

It was *my* life, after all, and *my sister's.* His lies meant I couldn't trust the man in charge of orchestrating both of those lives in the way he saw fit.

"Avarie, please talk to me," he'd said through the door, but until he apologized and told me the truth, I had no intention of opening the door or talking to him.

I heard a knock. "Hey, Ava. It's Saylor."

What was I supposed to do now? I couldn't ignore her. I walked over, unlocked it, and held it open for Razor's sister.

"Okay for me to come in? I come bearing gifts of clothing."

I smiled. "As long as Razor isn't with you, it is."

Saylor laughed. "Oh boy, he is in *trouble*."

I sat down on the bed. "I feel terrible about hiding out in here, but he made me so mad."

"Can I ask what he did?"

"He lied to me."

"I told him that's why you were pissed."

"Are the girls with you?"

Saylor nodded. "So is my mom."

"Oh, God. Does she think I'm the rudest person ever?"

"Nah. She took the girls down to the lake so I could straighten out my baby brother. They'll be back up soon."

"How did you get my clothes?" I asked when she opened the duffel bag.

"That hotter-than-all-get-out Monk left them for me at a secret location in town. God, I feel like a spy myself. It's pretty cool."

"Would you mind if I changed?" I asked, looking down at my sweaty, dirty t-shirt and shorts.

"Go right ahead, I'll hold the wolves at bay."

"The wolves?"

"My girls have talked about little else but 'Aunt Ava' since the day they met you. I don't know why they started calling you their aunt. I hope it doesn't bother you."

"No, it doesn't." I actually thought it was sweet.

"They're convinced that Razor is going to ask you to marry him, and you are going to ask them to be flower girls in your wedding."

I smiled when Saylor rolled her eyes.

"I may be way overstepping, but you do know he's in love with you, right?"

I took a deep breath and let it out slowly. "Did he tell you to say that?"

"Good God, no. I saw it straight away. He's head over heels, girlfriend."

I shrugged.

"And you love him too."

"It's crazy, but I do," I murmured.

Tabon knocked and then slowly opened the door. "Can I come in?"

Saylor looked at me, and I nodded.

"I'll be able to hold them off for ten minutes tops. If you're going to change, do it now." Saylor slipped out the door and closed it behind her.

"I'm sorry," Tabon said once his sister was out of the room.

"What are you sorry for?" I asked, hoping he'd tell me the truth, because if he lied again, we were going nowhere.

"I lied to you. I had a good idea who was following us, and why."

"Why didn't you just tell me that?"

"It's complicated, Avarie."

"Was it the people who have my sister?"

Tabon scrubbed his face with his hand and nodded.

"Is there anything else you can tell me, Tabon?"

He raised an eyebrow. "Tabon?"

"Answer my question."

"No, Avarie. There's nothing else I can tell you."

"Okay. Now, go. I'll be out in a minute."

"Why do I have to leave?"

"Because I'm going to take a quick shower and change my clothes."

"So?"

I put my hands on my hips. "Don't push me, *Razor*."

I saw Tabon and his sister sitting on the front steps, and the girls and their grandmother walking up from the lake in the back. I slipped out the door by the kitchen and waved at them.

"Aunt Ava!" both girls shouted and ran toward me.

"Well, hello," said Tabon's mother. "I'm Sally."

"I'm Ava, and it's nice to meet you. I'm sorry I wasn't out front when you arrived."

Sally tucked my arm in hers. "Did he apologize?"

I laughed. "So you know?"

"I know that you only call him Razor when you're mad at him, otherwise you call him Tabon."

"I'm so embarrassed."

"Don't be. I think it's adorable."

"Grandpa's name was Tabon, too," Sierra told me, coming up to take my hand. "Why don't we call Uncle Razor 'Tabon'?"

"When your Grandpa was still alive, it was confusing calling him and your uncle the same name."

Sally leaned closer to me. "Not that 'Grandpa' would've been thrilled with that name either."

"I told Saylor my mother won't even let my sister and me call her 'Mom.'"

"No?" Sally laughed.

"We have to call her Peggy. If we don't, she doesn't acknowledge we've spoken."

"Goodness. Well, that's…different."

"You don't have to be so nice. It's weird. And really awkward."

"What about your father?"

"He's good with 'Dad,' thankfully. He has other issues, though."

"Is it rude of me to ask what?"

"No." I laughed. "His thing is wives. With each divorce, they get younger. My sister and I are a year older than wife number four, who is the current one. Well, she was last week. It's hard to keep up."

Sally laughed too. "Oh, sweet girl. How did you turn out so lovely and…normal?"

"My sister and I kind of raised ourselves," I answered, blinking away my tears.

"Did I say the wrong thing? I'm so sorry."

"It isn't that. My sister…" I looked up at where Tabon sat with Saylor. "The truth is, I'm not sure I'm allowed to say anything."

"It's okay," said Sally. "I'm used to it. I used to think that Razor told me he couldn't talk about things so he didn't have to tell me the truth. Now, I've accepted that when he says he can't, there must be a good reason."

34

Razor

"She'll be out shortly," I told my sister.

 "There she is." Saylor pointed.

I looked up and saw her with my mom down by the lake with Savannah and Sierra. "How's Ya-Ya?"

"She's okay. She hasn't been up here since Dad died."

"Who has been?"

"Me. I bring the girls up here sometimes. I want them to know things about him, ya know?"

A week ago, I wouldn't have understood why. Now, though, I felt the same way with Ava. I wanted her to get to know my family, and that included my father.

"I told her you love her."

"*What?* What the hell, Saylor?"

"Are you telling me you don't?"

I shook my head. "What did she say?"

"I told her she loves you too."

"Are you kidding me? What is wrong with you?"

"Ask me what she said next."

"I'm asking."

"She said, 'I do.'"

"Is it crazy, Sayl?"

"She asked that too."

I looked back over at Ava talking to my mom. Maybe it was crazy, but I wouldn't change it even if I could.

"By the way, thanks for the phones, Sis."

"You're welcome. Although you should thank Monk, or maybe I should." She wiggled her eyebrows. "I'll go rescue Ava from my girls who are now probably asking to get fitted for flower girl dresses for your wedding."

I was entering codes into the phones and only caught the tail end of what my sister said. "Wait. What? My wedding?"

She punched my arm and walked away.

I shook my head and checked the phones' signal. Once it initialized, the first person I called was Doc, figuring he'd know the most about what was happening with Gunner and his team, and also with Onyx and Alegria.

"Where the hell are you?" Doc bellowed when he answered my call.

"Remote cabin in the woods, and safe, thanks."

"What the fuck, Razor? You asked Onyx to leave you by the side of a road?"

"I know what I'm doing, Doc, so instead of bitching at me, tell me what's happening."

"I'm still pissed about your tactics, but I will brief you on what's gone down."

Doc told me that Ivashov's intel on the Armenians was credible, and that while they hadn't been able to pinpoint exactly where the girls were being held, they believed they were close.

"And my team?"

"As much as I don't want to admit it, you were right. Onyx said they picked up the black SUV tailing them shortly before they arrived at the airfield in Florence. Once they got to the hangar, there was no sign of them. However, you know that means they're still looking for you."

"Roger that. Are we sure it was the Armenians?"

"As sure as we can be. We still haven't been able to locate Petrov."

"Any idea how he got to Finnegan?"

"When Striker first came to us with this, he said the agency believed there was an FBI agent in on it. My guess is whoever that is either killed Dash himself, or made arrangements for someone else to get access."

The work we did was damn hard, but when one of our own, someone we believed we could trust, turned on us, it made me want to seek them out and kill them myself.

"What about Monk?"

"As you know, he's still in town, waiting for word on where the hell you are."

"He'll know soon enough."

"Yep," said Doc. "Your twenty just registered."

"I'll be in touch," I said before ending the call.

"You damn well better be."

When I came around the side of the house, I found Ava with my mom, sister, and nieces. She had on a pair of the jeans I'd bought her, along with a Yachats long-sleeve t-shirt that Saylor must've thrown in. With her sandy-blonde hair, she looked like she could be Savannah and Sierra's mom more than Saylor did with her dark-black hair like mine.

As I watched them from a distance, I felt as though my heart would burst. Yeah, the situation we were in was about as shitty as it could be. Ava was in far more danger than she realized; her sister and two of her best friends had been abducted by some crazy Armenians who meant to grab Ava instead.

On top of that, those same Armenians wanted to draw out and kill the twins' father, who wasn't Conor McNamara at all, like his two daughters believed. Instead, he was Makar Petrov, a Russian arms dealer who'd disappeared a couple of years before they were born, and was believed to be dead. Talk about a *clusterfuck*.

And still, my heart was full because I'd met the love of my life—Avarie McNamara. No matter what happened in the next few days, I'd never, ever let her go.

Once we knew Aine, Penelope, and Tara were safe, and Petrov was no longer a threat to either of his daughters, I planned to ask Ava to marry me, and I didn't intend to take no for an answer. When my sister told me that Ava had admitted to loving me too, I knew exactly how I wanted my life to play out—with her by my side.

"I am seriously outnumbered," I said, joining the five females who meant the world to me.

"You could invite Monk to join us."

"He already did," said the man walking out of the forest and scaring the shit out of all of them, except me.

"I told him we needed a cook," I said.

"Chef."

"Right. Mom, meet Monk. He's a chef, and Saylor has a mad crush on him. Monk, this is my mom, Sally."

The man stepped forward and shook my mom's hand and then turned to Saylor.

"I already know who you are," he said and winked, to which Saylor put her hand on her heart and smiled at me.

I smiled too, but in the back of my mind, I knew the idyllic scene before me was temporary. After dinner, Ava and I would be leaving again, and our time at my dad's cabin would come to an end far too soon.

"Your mom is great," Ava said when I sat next to her and handed her the new phone.

"I'd have to agree."

"Much more so than my mom. And your dad sounds like he was pretty awesome too."

"Amazing how forgiving memories can be," I murmured, leaning forward to brush Ava's lips with mine.

The look on her face was questioning, but quickly changed to the haunted smile I was used to seeing.

"They're sweet together," she said, pointing to Monk and Saylor.

"Yeah. About that, it's never easy for a guy to see his sister with someone he works with. At least I know Monk is a better guy than her asshole husband was."

This time Ava leaned forward to kiss me.

"Sorry," I said.

"Don't be. We all have people in our families we aren't proud of."

"Come here." I pulled her over to sit on my lap. "I need you close."

"Is everything okay?"

I thought about saying it was, but I'd be lying, and it seemed that was the worst thing I could do with Ava.

"We need to leave tonight," I told her.

"I think I knew that."

"I'm sorry."

"I'm the one taking you away from your family, Tabon."

I came so close to telling her that she was my family, and that as long as we were together, I'd be okay. But Ava wouldn't look at it the same way I did. I wasn't her family; her sister was, and until Aine was safe, there'd be no professions of love and no conversations about our future. There was still the chance, too, that Saylor was wrong, and Ava didn't love me as much as my sister thought, and once this ordeal was over with, she'd go back to the life she had before, the one that I wasn't a part of.

I looked over at Monk, who was staring at his phone. When the man's eyes met mine, I nodded.

Shit. Time to go already.

"I hate to cut the party short, but we need to leave."

Both my sister and mother looked shocked but only momentarily. Ava stood, but didn't move until my sister hugged her goodbye, followed by my mom and both of my nieces.

"Monk will grab your bag when you've gotten your stuff together, and then we'll go."

35

Ava

For the briefest of moments, I'd let myself forget the nightmare that my life had become, and was enjoying the conversation I was having with Tabon's family. I'd even allowed myself to think about how much Aine would like them, while pushing all the bad thoughts about what my sister was going through out of my head.

And then, just like that, I felt the rug being ripped from under my feet when Tabon said we had to leave. I knew it would be tonight sometime, but I'd thought we'd be able to have dinner at least. I'd barely had time to say goodbye to his family.

As if in a trance, I walked into the cabin. I'd taken my toiletries into the bathroom; Monk probably wouldn't think to grab them.

As I walked by the back door, something caught my eye. What was that? *Was that Monk lying on the ground? And was that blood?*

Before I could scream, a gloved hand covered my mouth and an arm wrapped around my waist, knocking the wind out of me.

"Not a sound, or the little girls will be next," a heavily accented voice warned. "Nod if you understand what I'm telling you."

I did as he said, praying that he'd just take me and leave Tabon's nieces alone. And what about his mother and sister? It was just like when I learned someone had Aine. I'd offered myself then, just like I would now. I wouldn't scream. I wouldn't fight. I'd go along willingly, praying no one else would get hurt.

The man led me to the back of the house and through the woods, but not in the direction Tabon, Monk, or I had come from.

The man shoved me into the back seat of an SUV, facedown. I could hear him talking to another man, but couldn't understand what they were saying.

"Go!" I heard one of them yell, and the SUV lurched into gear as the driver pulled onto the road.

"Tabon," I whispered as I felt a needle penetrate my thigh right before everything went black.

My head throbbed. Just opening my eyes seemed like it would be far too painful. I groaned and tried to move but I couldn't; my hands and legs were bound.

When I did pry my eyes open, I saw they'd put me prostrate on the back seat of the SUV, and it was dark outside.

"Well, well. The princess has decided to wake up," said a man in the same accent as the other guy.

I closed my eyes. They probably expected me to struggle, but I wouldn't. No matter what they told me to do, I would, until I knew my sister and friends were safe.

36

Razor

"Ava's really lovely," my mother said as she hugged me goodbye. "I'm so glad we got to meet her today, even though it was brief."

"I'll bring her back again soon. I promise."

Saylor mouthed "Sorry," as both of my nieces hung on my neck so long I had to pry their arms from around me.

"Bye, Bro," she said, hugging me equally as hard. "Take care of that woman, and no more lying to her." She wagged her finger at me, but the smile never left her face.

As I watched Saylor climb into her Jeep and drive away, a feeling of dread overcame me. How long would it be until I saw them all again? How long would it be until I could bring Ava back here? Never before had I hated my life as much as I did right now.

I went inside to see what was taking Monk and Ava so long. Maybe they'd wanted to give me privacy to say goodbye, but we really needed to get on the move.

"Avarie," I shouted. "Time to go, baby."

In the same moment I realized the cabin was completely silent, I noticed the back door was partially propped open.

I ran over and found Monk lying just outside of it. I knelt down, checked for a pulse, and found one, thank God, but where in hell was Ava?

I scanned the area behind the cabin. To the left, I saw where the grass had been flattened in an almost perfect path into the woods.

"Monk!" I shouted, shaking him.

The man groaned and opened his eyes, pointing toward the forest. "They got Ava. One of them nailed me from behind."

My heart pounded as I ran in the direction of the beaten pathway into the woods.

How could I have been so fucking careless? So stupid? I was a trained operative, and I'd let my goddamn guard down for five minutes, and now, the woman I was supposed to protect with my own life, was gone.

I saw a clearing and ran toward it. I came out of the woods just in time to see the same black SUV that I'd seen earlier, speeding away.

The Armenians had Ava and were taking her God knows where, while I stood by the side of the road, with no way to follow them.

"Doc, the Armenians have Ava. They fucking took her right from the cabin. Monk is down!" I yelled through the phone as I ran through the woods back to the cabin. *"They're at least five minutes ahead of me."*

"Raze, slow down. You're breaking up. I'm only getting bits and pieces of what you're saying."

Fucking cell coverage. *"She's gone. They have Ava!"* I yelled into the phone.

"Got it. Sending backup now."

When I came out of the woods near the cabin, Monk was already pulling up in his SUV.

"They went east," I yelled, jumping into the vehicle and slamming the door closed as Monk peeled away.

There were no turnoffs from this mountain road, until it hit the highway ten miles from here. Our only hope to catch them was speed.

My phone pinged and I grabbed it, thinking that it was Doc with an update. Instead, I saw it was from the tracker app.

"We've got her," I told Monk. "At least until they find her phone."

"We've got her," said Doc, calling back.

"We do too, but I doubt it'll be for long."

"Gunner just made contact."

"And?"

"When he and the rest of the team arrived, the girls were gone."

"But they'd been there?"

"Affirmative. His best guess is they missed them by hours. Razor, we need to—"

I disconnected the call. I knew what Doc was going to say, and I wasn't ready to hear it, or agree to it.

"It's the most viable option," said Monk, without turning to look at me.

"Just fucking drive!" I shouted.

I watched the app and knew the minute Ava's captors found her phone. Less than a mile from where the road hit the highway, the tracking device lost contact. We no longer had any way of knowing which direction the SUV would take.

"Fuck," I seethed, knowing I had no choice but to carry out the plan Doc would suggest.

"There's no point in trying to track them now," Doc said when I called back.

I knew that. In fact I knew every fucking thing my teammate was about to say.

I stalked onto the plane, not bothering to make eye contact with Onyx or Alegria. I heard voices and knew Monk was briefing them, but I didn't give a shit.

Walking past the two seats where Ava and I last sat almost brought me to my knees. Holding the seat backs for support, I made my way to the very back of the plane where there were two staterooms. I entered the one on the left, slammed the door closed, and threw myself on the bed.

I'd never been a praying man, but I'd sure as hell pray now. I had a lot to ask for. First, that the bastards who took Ava, didn't hurt her—or worse.

Next, that Gunner was working out where the Armenians had moved the girls, so when this plane landed, I could meet up with them and get into position, waiting for Ava's captors to arrive.

Last, I prayed that Makar Petrov had gone underground and had no idea where either of his daughters was. If he did, then we'd not only be dealing with the Armenians, we'd also have to keep Petrov from getting his hands on Ava.

Would he kill her? God knew. For now, the only thing keeping me from going completely mad was my belief that the Armenians wanted Petrov bad enough that they'd keep his daughter alive, at least until they found out what she had on her father. When that happened, she, her sister, and their two friends, would, without a doubt, be eliminated.

I hated leaving Oregon not knowing for certain if her captors would bring Ava to Washington, but my gut, along with Doc's, Gunner's, and even Monk's, was telling me that was what they'd do. I had to trust it.

My phone pinged with a call from Doc.

"Yeah?"

"I want you to know that I've asked Shiver to stay put in Eugene for the time being. We've identified the vehicle Ava was in via security footage along the highway. We've put advance-tracking into place, but so far, we haven't picked up anything."

"Thanks, Doc."

"I understand how difficult this is for you, Razor. Believe me."

Several months ago, Doc's wife, Merrigan, had been abducted by a known Russian assassin, Sergei Orlov. Rescuing her was a mission the entire team, the CIA, plus MI6 operatives had undertaken. There were few who could be as empathetic to what I was feeling as Doc could be.

"I appreciate it, and as hard as it is for me to leave, my gut is telling me to go just as much as you are."

"We have everyone on this except Merrigan and me. While she *cannot* get involved, I can. Say the word and I will."

"I'll keep that in mind. For now, all I ask is that you try your damnedest to locate the Armenians and Petrov."

"Roger that."

We're on the ground, I texted Gunner when the plane was taxiing in.

Within seconds I received GPS coordinates in response.

The adrenaline began pumping through my body like it did whenever I prepped for a mission, only this time, it wasn't just any mission. Its success or failure would have far-reaching ramifications for my own future. There were few ops that didn't involve risking my life, but this one risked Ava's, her sister's, and the lives of two of their best friends. There'd be no chances taken that weren't well-thought-out and planned.

I'd make sure Gunner and everyone else understood that. As soon as I arrived at the coordinates, I also intended to let the team know my word was final, even above Gunner's.

K19 carried tactical gear on the plane at all times, so I'd already suited up. Monk was in the process of doing so, and once the plane was parked, Onyx and Alegria would do the same.

If our assumption was correct and Ava's captors were transporting her to Seattle, they would only be about another hour out, two at the most. We didn't have a lot of time to put a plan in place, but we'd been under far tighter time constraints.

Dutch met us on our way in and gave us a rundown of what we were up against.

"There are six still on the ground here. There were originally nine."

Which meant there were three Armenians transporting Ava. Between K19 and the agency, we numbered eight. With Raketa, we were equal. I wasn't convinced yet that she could be trusted. It would be up to Gunner to change my mind.

"Hey, Raze," he said when I approached the stakeout area. "Did Dutch brief you on your way in?"

"Affirmative," I answered.

Under different circumstances, Dutch and Striker could have gone in and gotten Aine and the other two girls out already, even outnumbered two to one. However, if they had, the men who had Ava wouldn't bring her here, and finding her would be impossible.

"Any idea what the girls' condition is?" I asked.

"All three are actively moving around," Dutch responded.

"Gunner, got a minute?"

"Yep." We walked away from the others.

"Where are Striker and Raketa positioned?"

Gunner used a stick to draw an outline in the dirt and then pointed to different places along a circle's perimeter. "Here and here," he said. "We'll send Dutch and Monk out to join them. I want Onyx to stick with us and Alegria to go switch places with Raketa."

"Why? Isn't Raketa a better sniper than Alegria?"

"She messaged that she heard chatter about Petrov."

"Do you think that's why she's really here?"

"It's definitely crossed my mind more than once."

"What happens after she gets him?"

"Can't answer that."

"What about the Armenians? Any chance she's working with them?"

Gunner shrugged.

There was always a chance that any member of a crew could've been turned and had infiltrated a unit, however, with Ivashov's connections, former or otherwise, that risk was exponentially greater.

I took a second look at where Dutch, Striker, Alegria, and Monk were deployed to sniping positions. Gunner and I would be first entry, with Raketa and Onyx our only backup.

"Do you trust her?" I asked.

Gunner nodded. "As far as I can throw her."

Within moments, the Russian operative joined us.

"Razor," she said in a Russian accent.

"Raketa."

She studied me for a moment and then turned to Gunner. "My sources tell me that Petrov is not far behind his would-be captors."

"Do they have an idea how many he's bringing with him?" I asked.

Again, Raketa looked at Gunner. "Three or four, they believe."

"What's their ETA?" Gunner asked.

"Not more than thirty minutes."

Which meant the Armenians would be here in half that time. There were four men who would have to be taken out immediately upon the others' arrival with Ava. Her three captors would be next, followed by the two who were inside with the girls. All of this needed to happen without the four hostages being harmed in any way.

At the same time, those in sniping position had to remain at the ready in anticipation of Petrov's arrival.

"Bring Dutch back."

Gunner nodded and radioed the operative.

"Do they have night vision?"

"Negative," answered Gunner.

That didn't surprise me, although I was certain Petrov and his team would.

Gunner radioed the update on Petrov to the three remaining snipers, and then had a conversation with Raketa that I couldn't hear.

"What's happening?" I asked when she went back into the woods.

"We both agree we can use one more sniper. She's good, Raze."

Good, if she was on our side. Bad, if she wasn't.

The next fifteen minutes dragged on while I went over the entry plan again and again in my head. If the snipers failed to take down any of the four, it would be up to me, Gunner, and Dutch to do so.

"You and Dutch take first entry," I said, changing my mind about being on the outside rather than in.

"Roger that," both of the men responded.

"Go!" I heard Gunner yell at the same time I heard the sniper fire—four shots. Each hit their mark, killing the men standing guard on the outside of the house. Two more shots followed almost simultaneously when Gunner and Dutch stormed through the door.

What I didn't expect was to hear three more shots. *Where the fuck was Ava?* Had one of the snipers shot too soon? I raced around the makeshift structure where the other girls were being held, and stopped dead in my tracks.

There, only a couple of feet in front of me, stood the love of my life with her own father pointing a gun at her head. Four others had their guns leveled directly at me.

"Hold your fire!" I shouted.

Neither Petrov nor his men were wearing night optical devices. Given my slight advantage, I slowly inched closer to Petrov.

My eyes met Ava's. They were opened wide, and tears ran down her cheeks.

"Another minute and we would've been gone," Petrov taunted. "Now the choice is yours. We can leave with my daughter and no one gets hurt, or she dies."

"Dad! What—" She gasped.

"Silence!" he barked, tightening his grip on her waist and shoving the gun harder into her temple.

"Let her go," I said, creeping closer.

"Nyet," he said, emphasizing his long-since-gone accent. "I didn't give up my own life all those years ago, to lose it again now."

I saw the flash of the infrared pulse through my NOD and dove, knocking Petrov and Ava to the ground while instantaneously, the snipers took out the other four men.

"Move!" I yelled at Ava, as her father reached to where his gun had landed, but she didn't budge.

"No! Don't shoot him!" she screamed back.

Before I could react, another shot rang out of the woods, hitting just outside of Petrov's reach of the gun. It didn't appear he'd been hit, but the gun had been. There was no way of knowing from this distance whether it remained usable.

I raced forward, pulled Ava to her feet, and got between her and her father. I heard another shot at the same time I felt a bullet impact my side.

37

"*No, no, no!*" I screamed as Tabon fell to the ground. I watched in horror as my father stood, grabbed the gun that had been knocked out of his hand, and pointed it at me.

I dropped to the ground near Tabon and closed my eyes, knowing that in the next few seconds, I'd be dead. I laid my body over his as more gunshots rang out, but I didn't feel anything. *Nothing hit me.*

I looked up, expecting to see my father, either lying dead on the ground, or about to shoot me, but I didn't see him at all.

"*Call HEMS,*" someone yelled from behind me.

"Let me get a look at him, Ava," said Gunner, moving me away from Tabon. He checked for a pulse and then rolled him to his side. "*Get that fucking helicopter here!*" he yelled.

"*Ava!*" I heard my sister scream. I stood but kept my eyes on Gunner holding Tabon's listless body.

"You fucking hold on, Raze. You fucking hold on," I heard him repeat again and again.

Aine and I stood with our arms around each other and watched the helicopter take Tabon away. Gunner was with him.

"Let's go, Miss Ava," Monk said, ushering me to a waiting SUV.

"I need to go to the hospital," I said in a voice that didn't sound like my own.

"That's where we're going. We need to get you and your sister checked out."

He did his best to shield me from the carnage that lay along the pathway to the vehicle, and I tried hard not to look.

"Where are Pen and Tara?" I cried when I didn't see them in the SUV.

"They're already on their way," Monk said, gently grasping my arm and helping me inside. I moved over so Aine could get in next to me.

"I'll stay in the back with them," I thought I heard Monk say as he climbed in behind my sister. The man I recognized as the pilot got in the driver's seat. What was his name? Was it Onyx?

Everything around me seemed to be happening in slow motion, and something was wrong with my hearing. Voices were muffled, words were unclear, even my own.

I clung to Aine's hand, rested my head on her shoulder, and cried.

We were led into the emergency room and the first two people I saw were Penelope and Tara. We ran to each other, crying.

"I'm so sorry," I sobbed.

"We're just so glad you're safe. They wanted you," Aine said, which only made me cry harder.

"Let's go see the doc," said Monk, again ushering Aine and me away from our friends. I looked behind me before I walked through the door Monk held open, and saw that Pen and Tara were being taken into a room too.

"You can see them again as soon as the doc checks you out."

I nodded. At least Aine and I had been taken to the same room.

"What about Tabon?" I asked, resting my hand on Monk's arm.

"I'll let you know as soon as I hear something."

"What did they do to you?" I whispered to Aine, knowing I had to ask, but not wanting to know the answer.

"They kept us drugged with something most of the time," she said. "I don't remember much."

"I'm so sorry."

Aine squeezed my hand. "Stop saying you're sorry. This isn't your fault."

"It is," I cried. "It's all my fault. And Dad, God, I don't even…" I looked at Monk.

Aine's face paled. "What…about…Dad?"

"It was him all along. He was going to kill me."

Aine studied me. "Ava," she said, "what…are you…talking about?"

Monk stood and approached us, putting one hand on each of our shoulders. "There will be time for us to talk about everything that happened later," he said. "For now, let's make sure that whatever you were drugged with is out of your system."

"Have you heard anything about Tabon?" I asked him again.

Monk shook his head. "Not yet."

When the doctor came into the room, he asked Monk to step out, and someone brought another gurney in. They asked Aine and me to lie down while nurses took our vital signs and drew blood. The doctor examined me first and told someone to start an IV.

He moved over to Aine and said the same thing. Once he finished, he rolled a stool between us.

"Until we get the blood tests back, we won't know for certain, but I believe you were both given Rohypnol. You may have heard it called the date-rape drug. It isn't used as commonly as in the past, but is far worse in terms of side effects."

"Side effects?" asked Aine.

"They're different based on the amount someone has been given, but headache, confusion, low blood pressure, and slurred speech are what we see most often. You may experience tremors, and your reaction time may be diminished."

That explained why my voice sounded funny and why I was having a hard time understanding what others were saying.

"If my suspicions are correct and you were both given Rohypnol, the drug's half-life is between eighteen and twenty-six hours. We'll keep you both here at least overnight, and maybe longer, for observation."

"What is half-life?" asked Aine.

"The duration of action, but clinically it means the point in time at which the drug's concentration is reduced by half. In other words, when you should expect to see signs of improvement." He looked between us. "Any other questions?"

I rested my head against the pillow. I might have questions if I'd understood anything he'd said.

The doctor stood to leave.

"How are Pen and Tara?" Aine asked.

"We're keeping them overnight as well. The staff on the medical floor is working hard to arrange for you to have rooms side by side."

"Wait," I said before he could leave. "A man was brought to this hospital via helicopter. Do you know his condition?"

"I'm not aware of any flight of life arrivals today."

"What happened to him?" Aine asked after the doctor left.

"Someone shot Tabon. It may even have been Dad."

Aine rolled to her side.

"Start at the beginning, Ava. Tell me how Dad is involved in all this."

"Remember I told you that I'd found out something I shouldn't have…about Dash, and that I had to testify against him?"

Aine nodded.

"He asked me to meet him at a specific time, but I ended up taking a cab because I didn't feel like dealing with the subway, so I arrived early."

I told her how I'd seen Dash hand over several large manila envelopes to another man, who in turn, gave him a briefcase full of cash.

"How did you know it was cash?" Aine asked.

"Because he opened it and looked inside."

"What were you doing?"

"Hiding and trying not to make a sound. Believe me, if I thought I could leave without either of them knowing I was there, I would've."

"Then what happened?"

"When the other man left, Dash saw me. He grabbed me and started yelling at me, threatening to kill me if I told anyone about what I saw."

"How did you get away from him?"

I closed my eyes, remembering the events of that night. What had seemed like circumstance at the time, no longer did.

"Dash was pulling me toward the elevator when Dad rushed up. I was so afraid of what Dash would do, and so relieved to see Dad, that I didn't think about anything other than getting away from him. Dash, that is.

"Dad walked me out and called me a cab. He asked me again and again if I was okay, and I told him I was. I made up this story about Dash asking me to get back together with him, and I was so emotional because I turned him down."

I explained that a few days later, I'd been contacted by a federal prosecutor and was brought in for questioning.

"I was scared shitless, as you can imagine, thinking I was in some kind of trouble. Instead, they told me Dash had been arrested, and asked me what I knew about the events that took place the night I saw him with the other guy."

"What did you tell them?"

I groaned. "I didn't think it was much, honestly. But now that I think back about it, they were particularly interested in what Dad was doing there. I told them it must've been a coincidence and a lucky one for me. God, what if that was the start of all of this?"

"What do you mean?"

"Tabon told me that Dash worked for someone close to our family. I disregarded what he said because Dad never had any friends I knew of. Mom either."

"Did Tabon know Dad was involved?"

"He must have."

I remembered Tabon, Gunner, and Doc talking about our father at the wedding, and how I'd gotten a bad feeling watching them.

"When he met me at the airport that morning and talked me into staying in California, he said something about the case against Dash being a lot more complex than I thought, and that the CIA wanted the man he worked for more than Dash. He also told me that he'd been hired to protect me."

"Who hired him?"

"I think the CIA did."

"Oh my God," Aine moaned. "Do you think Dad had us kidnapped?"

"I have no idea but, Aine, he isn't who we think he is."

"Where is he now?"

"I don't know."

The door opened and Monk came in. Before I could ask, he said, "Razor is in surgery."

"How bad is it, Monk? Just tell me."

"He's critical."

An hour after Aine and I were moved to a room on the fourth floor, Kade and his wife walked in.

"Hello, love. How are you feeling?" Merrigan asked quietly, running her fingers through my hair.

"I'm so scared," I whispered.

She pulled a chair close to the bed, put the bed rail down, and took my hand in hers. "You've been through quite an ordeal," she said.

I shook my head. "It's Tabon."

She nodded.

"Have you heard anything?" I asked Kade.

"He's still in surgery."

"Try to get some rest," Merrigan said. "We'll be here, and will let you know as soon as we hear anything."

"They drugged me with something."

"Let yourself sleep, love."

When I woke again, the sun was shining brightly through the window. How long had I slept? I raised my head and saw Aine was still asleep. Merrigan was sitting in the room's recliner, asleep too.

"How are you doing?" asked Kade, who I hadn't seen sitting on the other side of me.

I put my hand on my heart.

"Sorry. I didn't mean to startle you."

"I'm okay."

Kade nodded; his eyes were hooded.

"What? Has something happened to Tabon?"

"He's in intensive care, sweetheart."

"Is he going to be okay?"

"He's on life support."

I lowered the bed rail and sat up. "I have to see him."

"Ava, that isn't a good—"

"What's happening?" asked Merrigan.

"I told Ava that Razor is on life support," Kade explained to his wife.

"I need to see him."

"Of course you do," she said, walking over and pressing the nurses' call button.

"Can I help you?" said a voice through the speaker.

"We need a wheelchair as soon as possible."

"Give me a minute," said the voice.

"I can walk," I told her.

"Hospital rules, I'm afraid," Merrigan said.

I avoided eye contact with Kade, knowing he might try to talk me out of going to see Tabon—not that there was any chance in the world he'd be successful in doing so.

When Merrigan explained why I wanted to be taken to the ICU, the nurse asked us to wait another few minutes. When she came back, she wheeled me to the elevator and took us up one floor.

"I brought your chart," she said. "Otherwise, they probably wouldn't let you in to see him."

"Thank you," I murmured.

"I'll be right back." The nurse parked me in the waiting room where Monk also sat.

"Any word?" Kade asked.

Monk shook his head. "No change."

A few minutes later, the nurse came back out. "I'll take you in now." She wheeled me up to the closed door of a room and stopped. "I'm going to warn you, it looks bad."

"Okay," I whispered.

"There are a lot of tubes and monitors attached to him. And a ventilator is doing his breathing for him."

When the nurse wheeled me in, I covered my mouth to stifle my cry. Tabon was barely recognizable beneath all the medical devices he was hooked up to.

"Do you want me to give you some time alone, or would you prefer it if I stayed?" the nurse asked.

"Alone, please."

I got up from the wheelchair, sat in the chair closest to the bed, and covered his hand with mine. "I told you once that I couldn't live without Aine. But, Tabon, I can't live without you either."

I rested my head on the bed, near his side. Tears streamed down my cheeks. "I love you so much. I have since the first time I saw you. And you love me too—Saylor told me you did—so you can't leave me."

I couldn't stop sobbing. I loved this man with all my heart, and because of me, he was lying in this bed, barely alive.

I felt a hand on my back, and eased up, brushing at my tears. When I saw Saylor, I jumped up and threw my arms around her.

"I'm so sorry."

"Shh," Saylor soothed. "Come with me. There's someone I want you to talk to."

I looked at Tabon; my time with him had been so short.

"We'll come back," Saylor whispered, taking my hand. "Oh, the wheelchair," she said when we were partway down the hall.

"It's okay. I don't need it."

"Are you sure?"

I nodded.

"There are actually two people I want you to talk to."

Saylor stopped at another closed door and knocked. When it opened, I saw Tabon's mother inside, talking to a doctor. Sally held out her hand, and I sat in the chair next to her. She'd been crying, like I had, but she had a smile on her face.

"Is this Avarie?" asked the doctor.

I nodded.

"Good." The man looked up at Saylor. "Now that you're both here, I'll tell you what I've just told Mrs. Sharp."

Sally held both Saylor's and my hands, squeezing them.

"Tabon's organs are all functioning, and we have significant brain activity, enough that we believe we can withdraw life support."

Sally smiled and looked between her daughter and me. "Isn't that wonderful news?"

"He's going to be okay?" I whispered, almost too afraid to say it out loud.

"I'm not going to lie. His recovery may not be easy or quick, but yes, I believe he's going to be okay."

"When can I see him again?" I asked.

The doctor looked at Sally.

"It's up to you, Ava. Saylor and I want to be with him when they disconnect the breathing machine. You don't have to be with us."

I squared my shoulders. "I want to be."

"There's a chance—"

I shook my head vehemently before Saylor could continue. "He's going to be okay."

The doctor led us out of the office and back down the hallway. "A respiratory therapist will be assisting me by disconnecting the tube from the machine. I'm confident that Tabon will begin breathing on his own immediately."

"Are you sure you want to be here?" Sally asked once more.

"I do, as long as you're okay with it."

When we walked into the room, Sally put her hand on Tabon's left arm and motioned for Saylor and me to do the same.

I held my own breath, watching as the breathing tube was disconnected. At the same moment Tabon took a breath on his own, so did I.

"Now what happens?" Saylor asked.

"We wait for him to wake up," answered the doctor.

"How long might that take?"

I was so relieved Saylor asked, because as much as I wanted to, I wouldn't have.

The doctor shrugged. "That's up to him."

We took turns taking breaks, so Tabon was never left alone. Kade and Merrigan had stayed with Monk, and told me they promised to give Aine, Pen, and Tara an update as soon as there was one.

"He's breathing and doing everything else on his own," I told them. "We're just waiting for him to decide to open his eyes."

I looked around the waiting room. "Where's Gunner?" I hadn't seen him earlier when the nurse brought me to this floor, nor the last time I came out for a break.

"He's in the chapel," answered Monk from the far corner of the room.

"Where is that?"

"I'll take you," offered Kade. "How are you holding up?" he asked as he led me down the hallway.

"Better now that I know Tabon is going to be okay."

"If you need to talk, I'd offer myself, but you'd probably be more comfortable with Merrigan."

"I appreciate that."

"Here we are," he said, motioning to a door flanked by two stained glass windows.

"Aren't you coming in?"

Kade shook his head. "I think he'll want to talk to you on his own."

"Gunner?" I said, slowly walking down the aisle that separated the rows of pews in the small chapel. He brushed his face against his shirt sleeve before looking up at me.

I got right to the point, knowing that if the situation were reversed, I'd want him to do the same. "He's going to be fine."

Gunner didn't say anything, but his expression looked hopeful.

I told him that Tabon had been taken off life support because the doctor believed he was ready to breathe on his own, and that all of his organs, including his brain, appeared to be functioning properly.

"Thank God," he whispered.

"Can I sit with you?"

He scooted over so there was room for me to sit beside him.

"He's been my best friend for a lot of years," he said.

"Tell me about him."

Gunner smiled and started talking. Thirty minutes later, we were still laughing at the stories he told about boot camp and some of their missions. He even told me about how Tabon had been feeling the morning of Quinn and Mercer's wedding.

"Razor was so nervous about seeing you. I've never seen him like that. He was already so crazy about you."

"It was the same for me," I murmured.

"You probably want to get back to him."

"I'd like it better if you'd come with me."

38

Razor

It was almost as though I could hear voices telling me to wake up, but I didn't want to. I was having the best damn dream about Avarie, and I didn't want it to end.

"Tabon?"

When I heard her sweet voice, I opened my eyes.

"I was dreaming about you," I tried to say, but my throat hurt like a *sonuvabitch,* and my voice was so raspy I wasn't sure she could understand me.

"Yeah?" she said, smiling through tears. "Was it a good one?"

I looked away from her to see if we were alone before I told her exactly how good of a one it was, and saw Gunner standing with his back to the wall.

"Welcome back," he said, also smiling through tears. I could only remember seeing Gunner cry one other time in my life.

"How long was I gone?"

"Not quite thirty-six hours."

"Shit," I said. "Is that good or bad?"

"You were in surgery for twelve of them."

I tried to touch my side, but I had too many wires attached to reach it. "Where'd it hit me?" I asked.

"Both lungs."

"No shit? That's got you beat," I groaned.

Gunner motioned to Ava with his head, and I looked at her beautiful face.

"I'll give you two a moment," said Gunner, leaving the room. "Not too long, though. Your mom and Saylor will be back here as soon as I tell them you're awake."

"In that case, there's something I need to tell you. Come closer," I said to the woman who was my reason for living. "I love you, Avarie."

"I love you, Tabon."

Every time she tried to leave so other people could come and see me, I refused to let Ava go. As much as I didn't want to now, eventually, I knew I had to let her go. The nurses were refusing to let her sleep in the ICU until the doctor released her from hospital care, which wouldn't be until the next morning.

"Goodnight," she said as I pulled her in for another kiss.

"I don't want you to go." I wound my fingers in her hair.

"Ahem," said Doc, standing in the doorway.

"Yeah, yeah. Okay, I'll let you go, but only if you promise to sneak back up here in an hour or so."

Ava smiled, kissed my forehead, and waved at Doc on her way out.

"Your mother said the doctor warned her that your recovery might be slow."

I smiled. "He doesn't know me."

Doc laughed. "I said exactly that."

"Catch me up."

"You sure you're ready?"

I nodded. "Where the fuck is Petrov, and who the hell shot me?"

"I don't know, but we're working on it."

"The bastard got away? *Jesus.* How?"

"Someone helped him, but we aren't one hundred percent sure who."

"Who shot me? Do you think it's the same person?"

Doc nodded. "We do."

"You said not one hundred percent, but you have a theory."

"Gunner disagrees."

"Raketa-fucking-Ishakov?"

"Yeah, but it's Ivashov."

"I don't give a fuck what it is. I knew that goddamn bitch couldn't be trusted. She almost fucking killed me."

There was a rap at the door and Merrigan slipped inside. "We can hear you all the way down the hall-way. You have two choices: you can lower your voice and Doc can stay, or you can continue making the rest of the patients very uncomfortable and he can leave. What'll it be, Sharp?"

I closed my eyes and let my head rest against the pillow. "So she's gone?"

Doc nodded. "And so is Petrov."

"I would've killed him."

"I would've too if I'd been there."

"Ava stopped me, not the gunshot."

"I know."

"Who told you?" I asked.

"Ava did."

Shit. Which meant, even though she'd been all smiles while she was with me, she blamed herself for me getting shot and almost dying.

"This isn't Ava's fault," I said to both Doc and Merrigan.

"No one thinks it is, Razor."

"She does."

"I'm working on that."

"Yeah? Are you using your persuasive powers, Fatale?"

"I'm handling it like I would any other witness turned victim. It'll take time, but eventually she'll accept that her being in the wrong place at the wrong time doesn't make anything that happened her doing."

"Have you talked to her about her father?"

Merrigan looked at Doc.

"No," Doc answered.

"What was that about? Why'd you look at him, Fatale?"

"Because Merrigan won't let me talk to Ava about him."

"She isn't ready, Tabon."

"Ava's the only one who calls me that."

"Sorry. I meant Razor." She smiled. "Regardless of what your name is, Ava isn't ready, particularly since we don't know where he is."

"She knows he's gone. I guarantee it."

Merrigan nodded. "We haven't confirmed it."

"I wanna talk to Gunner."

"He's gone to the hotel," said Doc.

"I don't give a fuck. I want him here. Now."

Merrigan rested her hand on my arm. "If you keep this up, they won't let anyone in to see you, and they'll also sedate you."

I shook my head and rested it back against the pillow. "I need to see him," I repeated.

"I'll see what I can do," said Doc.

"I don't care if you and Monk have to knock him out and drag him here. I want to see him. Tonight."

"Where the fuck is Ivashov?" I spat at Gunner when he walked through the door.

"I don't know."

"She almost killed me."

"We don't know that. In fact, I'm positive it wasn't her."

"Why?"

"Wrong caliber."

"They recovered the bullet?"

Gunner pulled it out of his pocket. "The surgeon dug it out of you."

"I don't even want to know how you got it."

"Part of an attempted murder investigation."

"If it wasn't Raketa, where is she?"

"I'm afraid that whoever shot you, took her."

I nodded. One thing that Gunner and I had always agreed to do was listen to each other, even when we were fighting mad, even when we couldn't be further apart in our opinions. I respected the hell out of him, and if Gunner believed Raketa wasn't the one who shot me, then I did too. It helped a lot that he had the bullet that almost went through me, though.

"Petrov is still out there," I said.

"I know."

"That means Ava isn't safe."

"She is now."

"Yeah?"

"Striker, Dutch, Onyx, Alegria, Monk, Doc, and Fatale are all here. Fatale is here more as the mother hen, but I can guarantee you she's armed. Plus me, and Shiv is on his way with two more from MI6."

"Shit. All the big guns."

"There ain't no one gettin' to Ava McNamara, her sister, or the other two."

"The other two? You don't even know their names? Wasn't it a week ago that you were ready to…how'd you put it?"

"Don't remind me. And yeah, I know their first, middle, and last names, their damn social security numbers, and all other kinds of shit I shouldn't know."

I laughed and then winced.

"What did I miss?"

"Avarie was pissed at me about somethin' and asked if I knew her bra size and when she had her last menstrual cycle."

"And?"

"I told her I didn't but I knew when she lost her virginity."

"How are you still alive?"

"I'm charming."

"I don't think it's that."

I smiled, but then got more serious. "She loves me."

"Wouldn't take a former CIA agent to figure that out."

"I'm gonna ask her to marry me."

"Wouldn't take an agent to figure that out either."

"You know what this means, don't you, Gunner?"

My friend nodded. "We have to find Petrov and annihilate him."

"As soon as possible."

"Who should I take?"

"Dutch and Shiv, plus whoever Shiver brings with him, but ask Striker to bring in a few more. If you think we need it, ask Merrigan to contact MI6."

"Roger that." Gunner got up to walk out. "I sure am glad you're okay, Tabon."

I smiled. "Nobody calls me that but her."

"Yeah, yeah."

39

Ava

"How is he?" Aine asked when I got back to the room; Penelope and Tara were there too.

"He's *great.*"

"We're so relieved, Ava," said Pen. "We've been praying like crazy."

"It worked." I smiled and sat on the bed. "I'm so tired." I pulled back the blanket and sheet. "You don't mind if I sleep for a while, do you?"

"Of course not," said Pen, jumping up.

I crawled under the covers.

"We'll give you a hug and go," said Tara. "We're right next door if you need us."

"You're being too nice to me. What you all went through was so much worse." I looked at my sister.

"What we all went through was hell, Ava. And now we're here and together, and the doctor says we're going to be fine," Pen told her.

"They've arranged for therapists to come and talk to us before we leave too," said Tara.

"Get some rest," said Pen, kissing my forehead. "We'll talk in the morning."

"Are you okay?" I asked Aine after they left.

"What if Dad comes back for you?"

I wished I could tell her he wouldn't. I wished I wasn't just as worried as she was that he would.

"We need to chat," Tabon said to me when I talked the nurse into letting me go upstairs and have breakfast with him.

I sat down in the chair by his bed. "Okay."

Tabon tried to sit up and winced. *"Shit."*

"Jeez. Let me raise the bed."

"I gotta warn you, I'm not a good patient."

"That surprises me," I deadpanned.

"Come here, woman." He grabbed me around my waist.

"Don't hurt yourself."

"I love you, Avarie."

"Is that what you wanted to chat with me about, because I already knew that. Saylor told me before you did."

"I wish it were."

I sat back down, knowing full well that what he had to say was nothing to joke about.

"Go ahead."

"Your father."

"Who is he, Tabon?"

When he finished telling me what they'd suspected and confirmed about my dad, I felt sick to my stomach.

"What about my mom? Is she involved?" I asked.

"We don't have any proof indicating she is or was. She has her own detail, not that she knows it."

"Do you think she's in danger?"

Tabon shook his head. "No, but we aren't taking any chances. Not with any of you."

"What does that mean?"

"We'll have a lot of company, around the clock. Not just Monk, but others."

"That woman?"

Tabon smiled. "How many times do I have to tell you that I didn't have sex with Alegria?"

"Not because she didn't want to."

"You better not let Onyx hear you say that."

"Really?"

"No. I'm kidding. At least I think I'm kidding. You know what? I really don't care. My primary concern right now is your safety."

"What about my sister?"

"Aine, Penelope, and Tara won't be alone either."

"Have that woman watch them."

"You're jealous."

"Damn right, I am."

"I don't think anyone's been jealous over me before."

I rolled my eyes. "Sometimes I think you should rethink your chosen career field."

"That's something Gunner would say." Tabon laughed out loud and then winced again, holding a pillow to his side.

I stood and tucked another pillow under his head. "Be careful," I murmured. "He was so worried about you."

"He called me Tabon last night."

"Maybe everyone will start calling you Tabon."

"Nah, I told him I only let you do that."

I sat in the chair again and held his hand. "I love you so much. When you were…you know…on life support, I came and talked to you." My eyes filled with tears, but there was nothing I could do to stop them from falling. "I told you I couldn't live without you, Tabon. I told you not to leave me."

"Does it sound crazy that I think I knew that?"

"One of the nurses told your mom, Saylor, and me to keep talking to you."

Tabon closed his eyes. "It wasn't any different for me."

"What do you mean?"

"When Petrov had you…"

"My dad."

"I can't think of him that way."

It was hard for me too. Merrigan warned me that what I'd gone through hadn't hit me yet, and it would be hard to know when it would.

"I'm here for you," she'd said. "And if you don't feel comfortable talking to me, we'll find someone else."

I remembered thinking at the time that Merrigan was going to make a great mother. The comfort I felt with her was something I'd never experienced with my own mom.

"Hey," Tabon said, pulling my arm.

I sat on the side of the bed and rested my head on his chest. "I don't want to hurt you," I murmured.

"I don't want you to hurt," he said, stroking my hair.

40

Razor

"They're moving you to a regular room, Bro," said Saylor. "The doc said you're a damn superhero."

"I've been telling you that since we were kids."

Saylor slugged me and then sat in the chair by my bed. "How's Ava?"

"Fragile."

Saylor nodded. "Understandably."

"How much do you know?"

"More than you want me to."

"Monk decided now would be a good time for him to start talking?"

Saylor laughed. "No. Merrigan. How badass is she, by the way?"

I nodded. I guessed that Saylor actually had no idea just how badass Merrigan "Fatale" Shaw-Butler actually was.

"Ava's father remains a threat."

"What can I do?"

There really wasn't anything anyone could do but keep Ava safe until we found him.

"When this is all over, I'm going to ask her to marry me."

"Don't wait, Raze."

"No?"

Saylor shook her head. "You, of all people, should know just how precious life is. Ask her today. Hell, marry her today if she'll have you."

"Hey, how's Mom doin'?"

"Fine. Didn't you see her a half hour ago?"

"Yeah, but you know how she is."

"She's been a trooper. I have to admit, I was a little surprised."

Nothing our mom did ever surprised me. Talk about badass, my mahjong-playing mom would've given Fatale a run for her money if she'd decided to be an operative when she was younger.

"She likes Ava, right?"

Saylor's eyes filled with tears.

"What?"

"She asked her to be here with us when they took you off life support."

"Wow."

"I know."

"Just to confirm, that means she likes her. Right?"

Saylor slugged me again. "You're such a dork. How'd you ever become a spook?"

"Why do people keep saying that to me? And, by the way, we refer to ourselves as officers, not spooks."

"The plane is at the airfield," Onyx reported.

"Who's flying with you today?"

"Mantis."

"He's back?" The last I'd heard, Gehring "Mantis" Cassman was deep undercover in Afghanistan.

"Yes, sir. Ready to do nothing but fly planes for a while."

"I hear that. Did my sister get everything ready?"

Onyx laughed. "Yes, sir. She sure did."

"Good."

I checked my bag for a second time while I waited for Ava to come back with the wheelchair. I could damn well walk out of here on my own, but they insisted it was hospital policy that I didn't.

"I heard you were leaving today," said the ICU doctor. "Best of luck to you. You're definitely one for the record books."

"I had a lot to live for," I said when Ava walked in.

"Ready?" she asked.

"Never more ready."

"Tabon," Ava said when we walked out the front door, "is this really necessary?"

Based on the line of black SUVs parked near the hospital's entrance, one would think a foreign dignitary was coming or going. I didn't care. As long as Petrov eluded us, I wouldn't take a single chance with Ava's life.

I stood and winced. How was it that when I was confined to my hospital room, I felt fine, and now I felt like I'd been shot all over again?

"Are you okay?" Ava asked. "Do you need help?"

"Slide in ahead of me, baby," I told her and motioned for Monk to come closer. "Just in case," I muttered to him.

Thankfully we had more than adequate people working this detail, because I wouldn't be good for shit for quite a while, and I wasn't too proud to admit it.

"What's going on?" Ava asked when I led her to the rear of the airplane.

"There are staterooms back here," I said, wiggling my eyebrows.

I opened the door, and Ava gasped.

"Oh my God," she said. "It's so beautiful."

My sister had really outdone herself. There were strands of twinkle lights hanging in rows from the ceiling, the bed was strewn with red rose petals, and there was a bottle of champagne on the table, chilling in a bucket.

I led Ava inside. "Have a seat," I said, motioning to a chair by the table.

It wasn't easy, but I was determined to do this right. I put one hand on the bed, the other on the second chair, and lowered myself to one knee.

Ava gasped for a second time. "Tabon?"

I reached inside my pocket and pulled out a small box. "I never dreamed I'd find anyone who I loved even half as much as I love you. I can't live without you, Avarie. What's more, I can't live without you by my side. I'm asking, begging, pleading, imploring—will you marry me?"

Ava slid off her chair and put her arms around me. "Yes, I'll marry you," she said, scattering kisses all over my face.

"I wish I could say we should make good use of this bed, but I think all I'm good for is holding you, baby."

Ava smiled and helped me up. "I'm good with that."

"I didn't screw this up, did I?"

"Tabon, you asked me to *marry* you. There's literally no way to screw that up."

"Really?"

"Yes, really."

"I'm pretty good at lying on a bed," I said as she propped pillows behind me and then snuggled close.

"Hey, Tabon?"

"Yeah, Avarie?"

"Do you have a ring in that box, or was it just a prop?"

41

Ava

Every time I thought about his proposal and looked down at the beautiful ring Tabon gave me, I smiled.

He'd been mortified that he forgot to give it to me, but when I dissolved in a fit of giggles, he eventually laughed too.

"What are you thinking about?" he said, coming up behind me and kissing my neck.

"How much I love you."

"Saylor called to remind us that she's bringing the girls over today."

I clapped my hands. "They're going to be so excited."

"Do I…uh…have to do anything?"

"No. In fact, it would be best if you made yourself scarce for a while."

He pretend pouted and kissed my neck again. "They won't be here for another hour."

I slid off the barstool and took Tabon's hand. "Oh, look." I stopped on the way to the bedroom, and pointed at the whales whose blow I'd just spotted.

"I think you like it here."

I turned around and studied him. "I love it here, Tabon."

"Do you think you could live here?"

"Where else would we live?"

He shrugged. "It isn't New York City."

"We wouldn't be able to have sex in the middle of the afternoon with all the blinds and windows open if we lived in New York City."

"You make a good point."

Tabon lowered me on the bed. "I want these off," he said, unfastening the buttons on my shorts.

I lifted my bottom up, and he pulled them off along with my panties.

"These are my favorite," he said, dangling the sea-foam-green scrap of lace on his finger.

I unbuttoned my shirt and shrugged it off my shoulders.

"I like this too," he said, lowering himself over me and running his tongue where the lace of my bra met my skin. When he yanked on the cup so his mouth could reach my nipple, my fingers twisted in his hair, holding him close.

"I do too," I breathed, arching my back when he moved to my other nipple.

"I can't wait, baby," he said, standing to take off his shorts and shirt. "Close your eyes," he said, knowing that seeing his scar still bothered me.

"Open," he said once he'd lowered himself above me. "I want you to see the look on my face, so you know exactly how good I feel when I'm inside you."

I whimpered when Tabon's eyes practically rolled back in his head.

"God, I love that sound," he shuddered, thrusting deeper into me. "Almost as much as I love how it feels to have you wrapped around me." He reached down with his fingers and toyed with my bundle of nerves.

"Tabon, I—" I couldn't say another word as an orgasm swiftly overtook me.

"What was that?" he said, smiling down at me.

"I love you."

"Mmm. I love you, my sweet Avarie."

He started moving again, slowly at first, and then faster and harder. "Come with me, baby." He thrust one more time and then pulsed inside me. I clung to him as the look on his face brought me back to the brink, and then let my pleasure spill over us both.

"Have you thought about where you want to get married?" Tabon asked as we lay naked in each other's arms.

"Do I have a choice?"

He shifted me off of him and sat up. "Why wouldn't you?"

"I guess we could get married here."

He smiled. "Please hold back your enthusiasm."

"It really doesn't matter to me, Tabon. All I care about is being your wife; where and when we have the ceremony is inconsequential."

He rested his forehead against mine. "Close your eyes."

I smiled and closed them.

"Think back to when you were a little girl. Tell me what your dream wedding looked like."

"On the beach," I answered.

"Well, there you have it." He motioned out the window. "What?" he asked when my face fell.

"I think we should wait, Tabon."

"When I was still in the hospital, I told Saylor that when all of this was over, I was going to ask you to marry me. She told me not to wait. We aren't going to wait either, Avarie."

"I know I just said that I didn't care where or when, but I do care who's with us. That's why I want to wait."

"Okay…" he said, raising his eyebrows.

"*Not* my father, obviously. But I would like my mother to be there, and Quinn."

He nodded. "That can be arranged."

"Have you talked to her?"

"Quinn or Peggy?"

"You just gave it away."

"To be honest, I've talked to both of them."

Would it be terrible of me to say I wished he'd let me talk to Quinn too? I missed her so much.

"What?" he said again.

"Nothing."

"You're mad you didn't get to talk to Quinn."

"I'm not *mad.*"

"You're not going to start calling me Razor?"

I swatted him. "No, but I do miss her. Maybe next time, I could talk to her too."

"Yeah, I can arrange that."

Tabon picked up his phone. "As much as I'd rather stay in bed naked with you for the rest of the day, we need to get dressed, baby."

"Right, your sister is coming over with the girls."

"That's right."

42

Razor

"Now," I mouthed to my sister who was sitting facing me.

She and Ava, who had her back to me, were head-to-head, looking at what I guessed were flower girl dresses.

"Do you know where Razor might have a tape measure?" I heard Saylor ask Ava.

"Maybe in his office."

"Can you go look?"

I peeked around the corner and saw the look of confusion on Ava's face and then heard her say, "Uh, sure."

"Perfect," I whispered, coming around the corner to open the front door. I kissed Quinn's cheek when she stepped inside.

"Hi," she smiled and whispered as well. "Over there?" She pointed to where Saylor sat at the bar.

I nodded and went outside, closing the door behind me.

"How the hell are you?" Mercer asked.

"Crazy in love, and thankfully, not dead."

"I heard you came pretty damn close."

"Yeah, but I'm a superhero."

"That's what I always say about you." Mercer clasped my shoulder. "Seriously, I'm glad you're okay, and I'm sorry I wasn't here to help."

"Do you think for one minute that if you get into trouble, I'll come back from my honeymoon to help you?"

Mercer laughed and shook his head. "Nope."

"Damn straight."

43

"His office was locked," I said, coming back up the stairs. "But Monk said there might be one in the garage."

When I got to the top step, I raised my head and screamed. *"Oh my God, I can't believe you're here!"* I ran over to Quinn and hugged her as hard as I could. "Have you seen the rest of the tribe?"

"No. Razor asked us to stop here first." Quinn smiled and grabbed my hand. "Let me see it."

"Isn't it beautiful?" said Saylor. "It belonged to my father's mother."

"Wow," gushed Quinn, studying the oval-shaped diamond surrounded by tiny rubies. "It's gorgeous."

"I know," I said, gazing at it. "He almost forgot to give it to me."

"What?"

Quinn laughed when I told her about Tabon's proposal.

"I can't believe you waited that long to mention it. Actually, I do. It's so like you."

"We're talking a minute or two, but the look on his face…oh my God, I laughed so hard."

"It's so great to see you happy," said Quinn, hugging me again.

I laughed. "Who would've thought we'd be first?"

"Not me. I mean, I never thought I'd be first."

"You're back so soon. I hope it isn't because of me."

"Nope, not because of you. I wasn't doing well, traveling."

"Why not? You love to travel."

Quinn patted her belly. "Morning sickness is kicking my butt."

I squealed and jumped up and down. *"Oh my God! I'm going to be an auntie!"*

"What?" shouted Aine, coming through the front door with Penelope and Tara right behind her.

I embraced my four best friends at the same time, just like we always did when one or more of us had been gone for a while. This was the way it had been since we were all seven years old. Thank God we'd always had each other because, for the most part, our parents weren't worth a damn.

When the front door opened, I gave Tabon my biggest smile. "Thank you," I said, walking into his arms for a kiss.

"We wanted to surprise you."

"I'm so happy right now."

"I hope what I'm about to tell you is going to make you happier…"

"Let me tell her," said Aine, bouncing over to them. "Peggy's on her way."

My eyes opened wide, and I looked between Tabon and my sister. "Why?"

"Because she wants to," answered Aine.

"Why?"

"Quit saying that. She…uh…*says* she quit drinking."

"Get the hell out."

"I will not. She said she stopped the day she found out that we'd been kidnapped."

I counted the number of days on my fingers. "It hasn't been that long."

Tabon put his arm around my shoulders and kissed my temple. "Let's say we give her a chance."

I huffed, trying to decide how I felt about him and my sister ganging up on me. "I don't think I could take it if it didn't go well," I admitted. "I mean, I want her to be at the wedding, but why is she coming now?"

"Let's see how it goes. You can always change your mind."

I looked into Tabon's eyes. "What do you mean?"

"She's here for a long weekend, that's it. If you're uncomfortable, we'll elope."

"Elope?"

"Yep. Come here."

He led me over to the window, where he pointed down to the beach. "We'll sneak off in the middle of the day with my best friends and yours, and have a secret wedding by the sea."

I turned in his arms and kissed him. "Thank you," I murmured. "I'm sorry my family—"

"If you want, Saylor and I can tell stories about my dad all night long, and then you'll never feel the need to apologize again."

"He really was a dick," Saylor shouted from the other room.

"What's a dick, Mama?" I heard Savannah ask.

Both Tabon and I were laughing too hard to hear how Saylor recovered that one.

44

Razor

"I don't think we should meet here," I told Gunner the next morning.

"I don't either. Got any ideas?"

"Actually, I do. My dad's fishing cabin."

"Onyx and Alegria will stay here with the girls, and Dutch and Monk can stay with Ava at your place."

I hung up and went to look for Ava, who was sitting by the window, looking out at the ocean.

"Catch any blows?"

"What?" she asked, looking up from a book.

"Sorry, I didn't realize you were reading."

"I wasn't really, or at least I haven't been able to concentrate on it."

"What's got you so distracted?"

"What do you think?" she said, rolling her eyes.

Both of her parents? Just her father? Or was she still anxiety-ridden about her mother's impending arrival? I didn't want to ask and inadvertently bring up something else for her to worry about.

"The team has scheduled a meeting this afternoon."

Ava nodded, but didn't ask any questions. On one hand, I was relieved. On the other, it broke my heart a little that some of the spunk had gone out of her. I leaned forward and kissed her forehead.

"Dutch and Monk will be here with you."

Again, she only nodded.

I pulled a chair closer to her. "Talk to me."

Ava's eyes filled with tears. "I'm not feeling sorry for myself," she blurted.

"Didn't say you were. So, what's got you crying?"

"It isn't like Quinn had her mother at her wedding. That had to be as hard or harder than me not having my father at mine."

"They're equally difficult."

"I hate those weddings where the bride has her mother walk her down the aisle. It's just stupid."

I nodded. "Who says anyone has to walk you down the aisle?"

Ava shrugged. "I'll just look so pathetic."

"Come here." I pulled her onto my lap and shifted so she could rest her head on my shoulder.

"We can do whatever we want to, Avarie. We don't even have to have an 'aisle.' All that matters to me is that we'll be married."

"That's all that matters to me too, but I know my mother. She'll want to go all out, have this extravagant and embarrassing affair. And honestly, I can't afford it. That's the other thing; I don't have any money, Tabon."

I knew Striker had asked the justice department to freeze Petrov's assets in order to make it more difficult for him to run. However, no one was foolish enough to think he didn't have money in offshore accounts.

Since Ava didn't have access to her bank account or credit cards, I wondered how much she actually knew of her current financial situation. To my knowledge, her funds hadn't been touched, not that it made any difference to me whether she had money or not.

"That's the last thing I'm worried about."

"It shouldn't be."

"Why not?"

"I'm sure you don't want to marry a woman who has less than five dollars in her pocket."

I stood and, in doing so, picked Ava up. I carried her into the bedroom, rested her body on the mattress, and then stretched out next to her.

"Would you have said no when I asked you to marry me if you didn't think I had much money?"

"Of course I wouldn't have."

"Why is it different for me with you?" I ran my fingers through Ava's hair and looked into her tear-filled eyes.

"I'm such a burden."

"Seriously? A burden? You're hardly that, Avarie. You're the woman who makes me want to get up in the morning and stop putting my life on the line every day. You make me laugh more than anyone I've ever known, and my family adores you. You love my home, and you appreciate all the things about living on the Oregon Coast that most people wouldn't even see because they'd be too busy bitching about the weather.

"You're smart, and honestly, hot as hell, woman. If I could spend every day of the rest of my life with you wrapped up in my arms, I would die a happy man."

"My family…"

"I love *you*, so how could I not love Aine? I don't know your mother, but my guess is, somewhere deep inside, she too is very lovable. As far as your father is concerned, tell me this—do you look at Quinn any differently because of her mother?"

"Of course I don't."

"Then, don't put that on me either. The truth is, for most of your life, he provided for you and you had no reason to doubt him. Right now, he's a man with his back to the wall. His life is about to implode, and that means he'll likely spend the rest of it in prison. He did this to himself."

"Do you think he would've killed me?"

"I don't."

"He said he would."

"Only because he knew I would choose letting him go over losing you."

"Aine thinks he'll come back for me. Maybe her too."

I hated that she had to live with that fear, but until we located Petrov, it was a fear I had to live with too.

"That's why we practically have you wrapped in cotton, baby. I'm not going to lie to you and say that doesn't worry me too. However, you have the best operatives from three different agencies looking for him in order to put an end to your fear and bring him to justice."

Ava put her arm around my waist and squeezed. "Thank you."

"You're welcome."

"When do you have to leave?"

I closed my eyes, wishing I didn't have to, but the truth was, I should've left fifteen minutes ago.

"About time," Striker said when I pulled up to find everyone waiting outside the cabin.

"Fuck off," I muttered. Were we really considering asking this asshole to be part of the K19 team? Who out of the current partners actually liked him? I knew Doc didn't.

When I walked up to the door, Gunner clamped my shoulder. "Easy there, big guy."

"You can fuck off too."

"Hell when it's personal, ain't it?"

I got the door open and invited the men inside. The last time I'd been here was when the Armenians took Ava. I didn't realize how much it would affect me until now. I felt physically ill. Maybe that's how Gunner felt all the time. Ava was home, safe. Lena was dead. Yeah, it was hell when it was personal.

"Gentlemen," said Doc, "take a seat so we can get started."

I watched as they all sat, except me. Doc commanded the room in such a way that everyone complied with his orders, even Striker, the man that K19 essentially worked for. Even Shiver, who outranked Doc in terms of how high he'd risen in MI6, did as he said. There'd been a point I'd thought about confronting him about it, but with everything that had happened, it didn't seem important anymore.

"Shiv," said Doc. "Why don't you brief the rest of us on what you know about Petrov?"

Shiver stood and opened his laptop. "From what we've been able to glean from MI6 sources, he's no longer in the country. In fact, it appears he's returned to Azerbaijan."

"What about Ivashov?" asked Gunner.

"She's with him—although not willingly."

"Any theories on who shot me?" I asked.

Shiver nodded and turned the laptop around. "Anyone recognize this guy?"

I did, so did Doc and Gunner.

"Rauf Evasov. Thought to have been executed by Azerbaijan's military as part of a mass wave of arrests made last year. The number of suspected Armenian spies killed is nearing one hundred, minus one."

"Double agent," added Gunner. "He wasn't part of our count."

I shook my head. "That's how Petrov knew where the women were being held. He was working with Evasov."

"Yes," said Shiver.

"If Petrov has returned to Azerbaijan, we're going to have a hell of a time getting to him," said Striker.

"He's got Raketa," said Gunner.

All eyes turned to him.

"You're suggesting we go in after her?" asked Doc, rubbing the back of his neck with his hand.

Gunner shook his head, but I knew the look on my friend's face better than anyone seated at the table, even better than Doc did. Gunner wasn't suggesting we go in after her; he was planning to do it solo.

"Taking down Petrov is non-negotiable," said Shiver, "at least for MI6. We've been working this op too long to let him go just because he's hard to get to."

"The CIA—"

"Fuck the CIA," Gunner said to Striker, pushing his chair back from the table and standing.

"Agency resources are unofficial," Striker continued.

Gunner looked at Shiv. "Are MI6 resources *official?*"

Shiver nodded.

"Then, I'm in."

"You've got eyes on him? Ongoing, I mean?" I asked.

"Affirmative."

"Any ties showing up back here?"

"I can answer that," said Striker. "CRM Allied has essentially disappeared into thin air. And, without Finnegan's testimony, the justice department has no case against 'Conor McNamara.'"

"What about the wife?" I asked.

Shiver turned his laptop back around. From where I stood, I could see the photo of the woman who had been with Petrov at the wedding.

"Damn," I mumbled as I read through the dossier on Adrine Shah, also known as Kelly McNamara. While she looked to be younger than Ava, she was actually closer to my age.

"She's with him," said Shiv. "Our guess is that she's more of a bodyguard than a spouse."

"Let's recap," said Doc. "Are you saying the agency is officially out?" he asked Striker.

"Officially, yes," he answered.

"What he's saying is that he's in," said Shiver, "and so is the agency, *unofficially.*"

All eyes shifted to Striker.

"You quit, or did they let you go?" I asked.

"Resigned, effective this morning."

"Over this?" asked Gunner.

Striker nodded.

I saw the shift in my friend immediately. Striker had just gained Gunner's respect.

"Again," said Doc. "Who's heading up this mission *officially*?"

"MI6," said Shiv.

"What about Dutch?" Doc asked.

"He's part of the team that will stay on the ground here. So is Monk," answered Striker.

"On behalf of the agency?"

Striker shook his head. "I don't need to say it again, do I?"

The meeting wrapped with a definitive list of those on the Azerbaijani team and those who would continue handling asset protection in the States.

Ava's friends, Penelope and Tara, would no longer be required to stay in Oregon, and neither would her sister. However, all three would have ongoing detail until the threat from Petrov was neutralized.

Neither Doc nor Mercer nor I appeared on either of the lists compiled at the meeting. Gunner and I had agreed with Doc that it was time to make official K19 partnership offers to Onyx, Alegria, Monk, Dutch, and maybe even Striker.

"See you later this afternoon," Gunner said before leaving with Shiv.

"Roger that."

"Retirement's looking more imminent," said Doc.

"Sounds good to me. Never could've predicted I'd say that."

"I'm going to make a prediction that Gunner will be next, once this op is over."

"Yeah?" I wouldn't lay odds either way.

"He would've gone in for Ivashov alone."

I laughed, maybe Doc did know Gunner as well as I did.

45

Razor

The scent of Jasmine perfume permeated the entryway of my house, alerting me that Ava's mother had arrived. However, I didn't see or hear her or Ava.

"Where are they?" I asked Monk, who was coming up the stairs.

"The beach. Dutch has eyes on them."

"Doc wants to meet with the two of you," I told him.

Monk held up his phone. "Got the message."

"It'll be good to have you as an official part of the K19 team."

"I haven't accepted yet."

"No? What are your conditions?"

"Whether there are rules about partners getting involved with other partners' family members."

"This ain't the agency," I said, slapping Monk on the back. "The only rules we have are, try your damnedest to stay alive while, at the same time, making sure your teammates do too."

"Then, I'm in."

I walked into the bedroom where I had a better view of the beach. From there I could see where Ava sat on the sand next to her mother. The two were head-to-head enough that I decided not to interrupt. Instead, I walked out to the deck where the steps from the beach led, and sat in the sun.

It had been years since I'd felt as at peace as I did today, and even then, I wasn't certain that I'd ever felt as whole.

"Hello, Peggy," I said when she came up the steps with Ava. "You look great," I said, kissing her cheek.

"Thanks. I feel great too."

"Hey, baby," I said to Ava, hugging her.

"I'm glad you're back. Peggy and I want to talk to you about something."

"Who?" asked Ava's mother.

"Sorry, *Mom* and I want to talk to you. Aine should be here shortly, along with Pen and Tara."

I wondered if anyone had told them yet that they'd be permitted to leave whenever they wanted to. And if they had, how Ava would feel about them doing so.

"Should we wait?" I asked.

Ava shook her head. "Mom and I think that you and I should get married tomorrow. Oh, and your mom and Saylor are good with it too."

I was stunned, but tried not to look it. I was all for it. The sooner the better as far as I was concerned.

"What about a dress?" I asked.

"I told my mother you would ask that. You're always so worried about what I'm wearing. Anyway, there's a dress shop in Newport. I looked online, and they have a lot of cute things."

"It doesn't have to be a traditional wedding dress, Razor," said Peggy. "You're getting married on the beach."

I laughed. "You're right." Evidently, Ava's mother wasn't pushing for an "extravagant and embarrassing affair."

"So?" asked Ava.

"Oh, are you waiting for me? Yes. I'm all in."

"I was thinking since everyone is here…Quinn asked Mercer to talk to Gunner and Doc, and they're okay with it."

I sat in one of the deck chairs and pulled Ava onto my lap. "I think it's a great idea."

"Thank God," said Saylor, walking out to the deck. "I don't know how much longer I can keep the girls from wearing their dresses."

"We went ahead and had flower girl dresses made for them," Ava explained.

"Hey, Sis," I said when she leaned down to kiss first my cheek and then Ava's.

"Get this," said Saylor, chuckling. "Mom asked Andie if she'd make a cake."

Ava gave me a stern look. "She isn't invited."

"You'll get no argument from me."

"Neither is the other one."

"You have one hundred percent control of the guest list, baby."

"You two need to get going," Saylor said, poking me.

"Okay. Where?"

"Marriage license?"

"What the hell do I know? I've never done this before."

"And you never will again," said Ava, kissing my cheek.

"Sure as hell won't."

46

"Are you sure you don't want to pick out your own dress?" Tabon asked on our way to the courthouse.

"Whatever Aine picks out will be fine."

"Okay," he said as though he didn't believe me, but it was the truth. I'd given it a lot of thought when my mother asked if this was really the type of wedding I wanted. When Tabon said we could elope if that's what I wanted, and then took me to the window and said we could get married on the beach with my best friends and his, it sounded so perfect that I couldn't imagine doing it any other way.

I didn't even care whether we had food or a cake, but agreed to let Tabon's mother and sister handle it any way they wanted to when they asked.

"What about me? Am I supposed to wear something…specific?" he asked.

"I've seen your closet; you have plenty to choose from. But to answer your question, I was thinking shorts and Hawaiian-type shirts might be nice."

"Let me guess, someone is getting those for us?"

I nodded. "Doc and Merrigan are in charge of that."

"How did things go with your mom?" Tabon asked when we pulled into the parking lot.

"Great, actually. Although…I have news."

"Yeah?"

"She kind of wants to live here."

"Kind of?"

"As long as you're okay with it."

Tabon's eyes opened wide. "With us?"

"Good God, no." I laughed. "The look on your face, though…even Aine doesn't want to actually live with her."

"Is Aine thinking of living here too?"

"Um…yeah."

When we rounded the corner to go into the building, Tabon pulled me into an alcove.

He grasped my chin and put his arm around my waist—just like he had in the garden at Quinn and Mercer's wedding—and covered my mouth with his.

"I was so afraid you wouldn't feel the same way about me as I felt about you," he said. "I guess that's how I knew it was love. Anything but spending the rest of my life with you wasn't something I'd let myself think about."

"I felt the same way, although it seemed like too much of a dream."

"I love you so much, Avarie."

"I love you too, Tabon."

Epilogue

Razor

"Doc just sent this." I handed Ava my phone. "He and Merrigan named the baby Laird."

"He's beautiful," she gushed, looking at the photo. "Do you want to wait to find out whether we're having a boy or girl, like they did?"

"I don't know. What about you?"

"I keep changing my mind."

I looked out at the moonlit waves crashing against the shore. It had been too long since I'd heard from Gunner, the man who was as close to a brother as I'd ever have. Reports coming in from the team searching for Ava's father were sporadic at best, but Gunner had gone completely dark, even to me.

Doc and I had talked about it yesterday. "It's like when you were gone. For every smile, there were ten tears, twenty moments of sadness, and even more of fear and uncertainty," I'd said.

"I know he wouldn't want us to feel that way. I certainly didn't want that."

"I *knew* you were still alive; I just couldn't bring myself to say it out loud. I didn't want to be wrong."

"How are you feeling now, about Gunner?"

"If he weren't alive, I'd know it."

"Me too."

"Are you thinking about Gunner?" Ava asked.

"Yeah. I'm sorry."

"It's okay. I think about him a lot too. You should talk to him."

I smiled. "Yeah?"

Ava nodded.

"He'll just give me a smart-ass response."

Ava walked over, sat on my lap, and kissed me. Nothing in the world felt better than having her in my arms.

"Tabon, what was your grandmother's name?"

"Which one?"

"Both."

"My mom's mother's name was Adelaide. And my father's was Louisa."

"Perfect. Adelaide Louisa Sharp. I love it."

"What if it's a boy?"

Ava raised an eyebrow.

"Okay, but we're never calling him Six."

Keep reading for a sneak peek at the next
book in Heather Slade's
K19 Security Solutions Team One Series,
Gunner's Redemption

He's a military hero falling for the enemy.
She's a Russian spy who wants out of the game.
With GUNNER by her side, can
she finally take her shot?

GUNNER

As a K19 Security founding partner, stealth is my middle name. Where I am is always need to know—even to my team. I like to keep it secret and discreet, so helping a sexy and mysterious woman from a dangerous Russian organization is right up my alley. But giving her my heart, may be more perilous than even I can handle.

RAKETA

I want out. I'm sick of living on the fringes, facing certain death every day of my life. I need to defect, and in order to do that, I must get help from a man who considers me an enemy. I've got one shot—one chance at a new life. Can I trust him enough to take it with GUNNER?

1

Raketa

"You shouldn't be here. What the fuck are you doing here?" Gunner scowled through what was obviously a drunken haze when I found him sitting in the otherwise empty bar.

"Paps, you're—"

"Don't call me that," he barked at me.

"Izvini," I muttered. "I know Lena was—"

In a flash, Gunner stood and grasped my neck with his hand, holding it tightly enough that it was difficult for me to breathe, but not enough that he cut off my air supply entirely. If I wanted to, it would be easy for me to break free. Instead, I absorbed the pain flowing from his fingertips.

"Never say that name again either. Do you understand me?"

I couldn't nod or speak with his hand on my throat, but my eyes bored into his.

"Never," he spat again, this time releasing me.

I sat down at his table when he did, and lifted the half-empty bottle of vodka. "May I?"

He grabbed it from me, stood, and stalked over to the bar. When he returned, he slammed a glass on the table in front of me and poured.

I threw the shot back and poured myself another. This time I waited for him since his glass was still full. My eyes remained focused on his as my hand clasped the icy-cold vodka.

"Leave," he said right before he threw the shot back.

I shook my head, watching the only other person in the room, the bartender, follow a command intended for me.

Gunner inched closer, leaning forward enough that I could feel the heat of his breath. "I want to be left the hell alone," he seethed.

"No." I'd been where he was too many times before, but never because I'd killed someone I cared about.

"Then, I'll leave." Gunner stood, tucking the bottle of vodka in the crook of his arm. He swayed just slightly, but caught himself and backed away before I could touch him.

"No," I said again.

He slammed the bottle back on the table and grasped my neck, this time from the back.

"You saved my life," I whispered.

"You would've lived."

If Gunner moved any closer, our lips would touch. Instead of waiting for him to do it, I brushed his mouth with mine.

"Fuck," he groaned as he wound his arm around my waist, pulled my body flush with his, and slid his tongue between my lips.

When I put my arms around his neck and pressed my breasts against his chest, Gunner put his knee between my legs.

"Take what you need, Rocket Girl," he taunted when I straddled his powerful thigh.

"Not here," I said as he moved his leg, backed me up against the wall, and put his hands beneath my bottom.

"Put your legs around me," he demanded.

When I did, he ground himself against me.

"Is this what you want?" he asked before bringing his lips to mine and kissing me in a way that no man ever had or ever would again.

About the Author

USA Today and Amazon Top 15 Bestselling Author Heather Slade writes shamelessly sexy, edge-of-your seat romantic suspense.

She gave herself the gift of writing a book for her own birthday one year. Forty-plus books later (and counting), she's having the time of her life.

The women Slade writes are self-confident, strong, with wills of their own, and hearts as big as the Colorado sky. The men are sublimely sexy, seductive alphas who rise to the challenge of capturing the sweet soul of a woman whose heart they'll hold in the palm of their hand forever. Add in a couple of neck-snapping twists and turns, a page-turning mystery, and a swoon-worthy HEA, and you'll be holding one of her books in your hands.

She loves to hear from my readers. You can contact her at heather@heatherslade.com

To keep up with her latest news and releases, please visit her website at www.heatherslade.com to sign up for her newsletter.

MORE FROM AUTHOR HEATHER SLADE

BUTLER RANCH
Kade's Worth
Brodie's Promise
Maddox's Truce
Naughton's Secret
Mercer's Vow
Kade's Return
Butler Ranch Christmas

WICKED WINEMAKERS
FIRST LABEL
Brix's Bid
Ridge's Release
Press' Passion
Zin's Sins
Tryst's Temptation

WICKED WINEMAKERS
SECOND LABEL
Beau's Beloved
Coming Soon:
Cru's Crush
Bones' Bliss
Snapper's Seduction
Kick's Kiss

ROARING FORK RANCH
Coming Soon:
Roaring Fork Wrangler
Roaring Fork Roughstock
Roaring Fork Rockstar
Roaring Fork Rooker
Roaring Fork Bridger

THE ROYAL AGENTS
OF MI6
Make Me Shiver
Drive Me Wilder
Feel My Pinch
Chase My Shadow
Find My Angel

K19 SECURITY
SOLUTIONS TEAM ONE
Razor's Edge
Gunner's Redemption
Mistletoe's Magic
Mantis' Desire
Dutch's Salvation

K19 SECURITY
SOLUTIONS TEAM TWO
Striker's Choice
Monk's Fire
Halo's Oath
Tackle's Honor
Onyx's Awakening

K19 SHADOW OPERATIONS
TEAM ONE
Code Name: Ranger
Code Name: Diesel
Code Name: Wasp
Code Name: Cowboy
Code Name: Mayhem

K19 ALLIED INTELLIGENCE
TEAM ONE
Code Name: Ares
Code Name: Cayman
Code Name: Poseidon
Code Name: Zeppelin
Code Name: Magnet

K19 ALLIED INTELLIGENCE
TEAM TWO
Coming Soon:
Code Name: Puck
Code Name: Michelangelo
Code Name: Typhon
Code Name: Hornet
Code Name: Reaper

PROTECTORS
UNDERCOVER
Undercover Agent
Undercover Emissary
Coming Soon:
Undercover Savior
Undercover Infidel
Undercover Assassin

THE INVINCIBLES
TEAM ONE
Decked
Edged
Grinded
Riled
Smoked

THE INVINCIBLES
TEAM TWO
Bucked
Irished
Sainted
Hammered
Ripped

THE UNSTOPPABLES
TEAM ONE
Furied
Merried

COWBOYS OF
CRESTED BUTTE
A Cowboy Falls
A Cowboy's Dance
A Cowboy's Kiss
A Cowboy Stays
A Cowboy Wins